ISBN: 979-8-9859829-7-8

Book/Cover Design by: **MATT DURAND**

Cover Photos by Sumeet Singh | Grant Cai | Set.SJ via unsplash

A DECLAN WYLER NOVEL

BRAWL DOGS

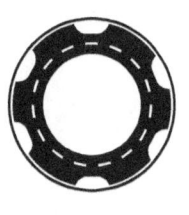

MATT DURAND

PART
1

Chapter 1

"Search," Declan Wyler said.

Blackjack, a tan and black Belgian Malionois, lowered his nose to the warm August Atlantic City sand and began to sweep it from side to side like a metal detector. Wyler gave some slack on the leash and then tapped a button on his smartwatch, enabling a custom-made map that would track their progress. A similar watch was strapped to a collar around his canine partner's neck. As they moved, the collar emitted a series of beeps and vibrations meant to assist the dog in finding his target.

Memories of Florida stuck with Wyler. The operation had led them into a firefight where Blackjack got separated from him and took two bullets to the leg as a result. Wyler's throat tightened remembering the panic that flooded him when he couldn't find his dog. Precious minutes were lost during his hunt, minutes that could have cost Blackjack his life. Ever since then, Wyler devoted his time and energy to creating a training regimen so they could easily find one another again should the need arise. The beach was a cumulative test of their months of training.

"Good," Wyler said. "Right track. Keep going."

The starting point he selected was relatively deserted. He wanted the distractions to gradually increase in difficulty. Blackjack easily went through the first half mile without issue, sticking close to the trail. After another quarter of a mile, they hit a heavily populated section of the beach. Now the real test began. Distractions littered the landscape. Waves crashing. Kids splashing. Seagulls squawking. Beer cans cracking open. Scents of suntan lotion melded into undercurrents of fried seafood. It was a minefield of people, each chattering in a cacophony of garbled conversations.

"Focus," Wyler said, as Blackjack paused to watch a wild toddler go streaking past him, sand spewing out from an overflowing bucket, while his red-faced mother gave chase. "Find the scent. Search."

Blackjack's highly tuned nose returned to the ground, sniffing vigorously. As he veered off track, the watches' pinging slowed, notifying him to redirect his path.

"Let's find the scent," Wyler offered for encouragement. "Keep going. Good."

Once Blackjack dodged an overturned tray of half eaten french fries soaked in ketchup, he appeared to lock back onto the trail. No matter how many times Wyler witnessed the feat, he couldn't help but be amazed. What it must be like to have senses that acute, he thought. Dogs were truly special creatures. Blackjack's pace quickened as he emerged through the thick field of tourists and New Jersey faithfuls. The pinging on the collar steadily increased, letting the dog know he was getting closer to his target.

"Good boy," Wyler said. "On scent. Keep going."

After another half mile, they approached a pier. The watch pinged like crazy, and Blackjack pulled against the leash knowing he was about to complete his task. As they entered the shadows, a woman appeared to their right, leaning against a beam. She was the target. Ellie Sloan, Wyler's girlfriend.

"Good boy," Wyler said as Blackjack excitedly sniffed and rubbed into Ellie's long bare tanned legs. Wyler produced a treat, which Blackjack quickly devoured for a job well done.

"I never doubted you for a second," Ellie said, scratching Blackjack's haunches with both hands. "How'd he do?"

"Got tied up a little when we hit the main stomping grounds."

"The Jersey shore has a way of distracting any sane mind."

"That it does."

Wyler led them to a patch of sand shaded by the pier, where he then poured water into a collapsible bowl for Blackjack. Wyler and Ellie sat down with the dog between them. Ellie caressed a spot near Blackjack's shoulders. Her legs bent elegantly as she dug her toes into the sand. A pair of white shorts covered a mere four inches of thigh. A fitted gold tank top hugged the roundness of her chest. Hints of a black lace bra peeked out from the edges of the tank. Her thick auburn hair hung in a loose ponytail. Ellie Sloane—Wyler determined the first day he met her—was one of a kind.

She tended bar at the Whitmore Club, where Wyler played poker. Every guy there had a crush or fantasy about Ellie of some kind. She was smart, funny, and easy to be around. Her laughter managed to patch over some of the cracks in his heart leftover from his ex, Enola—the one woman Wyler admitted to himself that he ever truly loved.

"I can't believe that worked," Ellie said. "How far was that?"

"A good two miles."

"How long did it take him?"

"Forty-five minutes."

"I swear this dog is smarter than half my regulars at the bar." Wyler smiled. "It's certainly possible."

"Two and a half miles tomorrow?"

"Sure."

Wyler reached into his pocket and pulled out a small, flat box. "Here, this is for you."

She gasped sarcastically. "A diamond already?"

"Not quite."

Ellie opened the box. She plucked out a smooth black device about the size of her thumb. The front side had a recessed circular power button in the middle, and the back had a thin screen.

"Oh, how thoughtful. You bought me a USB drive. Some girls get diamonds. Others get pearls. How lucky am I?"

Wyler laughed. "It's a transmitter." He pinched the stainless steel beaded chain around his neck and threaded it through the top of his t-shirt. An identical device dangled at the end of the chain next to his dog tags. "I've got one too."

"Okay?" she said, holding it up in front of her face. "And what do I need a transmitter for?"

"It syncs to Blackjack's collar."

Wyler pressed the power button on his device. "It sends out a signal so Blackjack can find us, like what we did today. And on the back..." Wyler flipped the transmitter over, revealing white numbers on the thin screen. "...it gives you Blackjack's coordinates, so we could find him if we ever needed to."

"Why wouldn't you just use your watch or phone?"

"I would. Think of this as a last resort. If the watch and phone die. This is for the worst case scenario. Or if something should happen to me."

Ellie turned her attention to Wyler instead of the device.

"And what might happen to you?" she asked, raising an eyebrow.

There were parts of Wyler's history he hadn't shared with her. Big, dark, violent parts littered with dead bodies. He had killed at least a dozen people overseas as a Marine. Those weren't the bodies that concerned him, though. Most people could, if not understand, at least accept to a certain degree, the actions soldiers took in service to their country but outside of that, it was a different story. In his civilian life, he'd racked up a body count that rivaled his tenure in the military. The men he killed hurt dogs. To Wyler, that was the only justification he needed for putting those men in the ground. And he would do it again if he needed to. He understood and accepted the ugly parts of himself. But would Ellie? That was the question he asked himself over and over again. The possibility of her seeing him as a monster kept him from opening up. He knew, eventually, he would have to if he wanted their relationship to work. It just wasn't a gamble he was ready to take at the moment. The transmitter, he hoped, would buy him time. It served as his way of showing her he cared and wanted her in his life.

"Lots of things can happen," Wyler grinned. "Sudden heart attack, car crash, eaten by a shark, human trafficking."

"Human trafficking?"

"I am pretty desirable."

"Fair."

"I hear alien abductions are on the rise."

"Okay. Okay. I get it."

"Nothing's going to happen," Wyler said. "But you never know."

"That's ominous. So in this worst-case scenario, I take it you're out of the picture? Does that mean you'd want me to take care of Blackjack?"

Wyler nodded. "If that's too much ... I understand—"

Ellie squeezed Wyler's arm as she stared into his eyes. "I'd do it in a heartbeat."

Wyler nodded again, then looked at the ocean. Ellie released his arm.

"I'd take you over a diamond ring any day of the week," she said, scratching Blackjack's head, resulting in a steady beat of tail wagging.

Wyler exhaled, grateful he'd survived the conversation.

"I bet he could go five miles," Ellie said, shifting the topic back to Blackjack. "His leg healed up nice. He doesn't seem to have any issues with it."

"Your delicate touch did wonders."

"That's funny. I was just thinking of a delicate place I'd like touched right now."

Wyler grinned. "If I didn't know any better, I'd say you were trying to seduce me."

Ellie rested her chin on her shoulder with a playful smile. "And if I was?"

Wyler stood and brushed the sand from his pants. He offered his hand to Ellie.

"Then I'd say we should get out of here."

Ellie took his hand and sprang to her feet. She leaned in close to kiss Wyler's cheek. Subtle scents of suntan lotion and salt cascaded over him. His heartbeat quickened.

"You're trouble, you know that."

Ellie smiled as she linked her arm with Wyler's. "Only the best kind, though."

"Yeah," Wyler said. "Only the best kind."

A notification ping woke Wyler from a lazy afternoon slumber five hours later. He untangled his limbs from a still-sleeping Ellie. After rolling onto his side, Wyler grabbed the phone from the nightstand. Two text messages waited for him from an unknown number. He unlocked the phone and read the messages.

(TS) What up, Big Dog. It's Soto. New phone. New number.

(TS) In AC for a bit of business and pleasure. U around for a drink? Catch up on old times?

Tomás Soto. It was a name Wyler hadn't heard in two years. They had met overseas as Marines during a joint offensive against a stronghold of Taliban fighters. A quick bond formed over their love of cards. Last Wyler knew, Soto was a real estate agent in Los Angeles. With no work obligations for the next three days, Wyler texted back.

(DW) What's good, Soto? Yeah, I'm kicking around.

(DW) I'll be at the Whitmore Club. 9pm. We can get a game in if you're down?

Wyler returned the phone to the nightstand and rolled onto his back. The text stirred up memories of first meeting Soto, who had been in Afghanistan six months longer than Wyler. Soto strutted around with a cocky assuredness that he gained from surviving a handful of near-death experiences. Wyler witnessed two of the experiences firsthand. One was a bullet that ricocheted off Soto's helmet. The other was when they were in a firefight in the woods. As Soto advanced, a grenade detonated four feet to his left. A tree absorbed the brunt of the blast. Had Soto been one step slower or faster, he would have been killed. Word spread throughout the ranks of the close calls. Some soldiers wanted to ride the Humvees with him, believing he was lucky. Others avoided him like the plague, not wanting to be near him, knowing his luck would eventually run out.

Wyler's phone pinged again. He read the reply from Soto.

(TS) I'll be there

(TS) Got an opportunity for you too

(DW) Opportunity?

(TS) Yeah. Easier to explain in person

(TS) See you soon, brother

The message piqued Wyler's interest. He hoped it wasn't an investment scheme or a sales pitch to get into real estate. Neither were paths he wanted to pursue. Ellie draped an arm over Wyler's chest and kissed his shoulder.

"Everything alright?" she asked, her eyes still closed.

"Yeah. An old buddy's in town. Wants to meet up. You working tonight?"

"Eight to two."

"Looks like you're going to have company."

"You just can't get enough of me, can you?"

"I find your modesty appealing."

He swung his feet out from under the sheet. Ellie tightened her grip around his chest.

"Where are you going?" she said.

"The guy I'm meeting likes to tell stories. I'm sure it's going to be a long night. Want to get a run in before I'm tied to a chair for hours."

She traced her hand down his chest over his stomach. Her

hand kept traveling south.

"I'm not done with you yet."

Wyler gazed over his shoulder. Ellie smiled and pulled him back into the bed.

At six, Wyler forced himself to his feet. If he stayed any longer, he might never come up for air.

"You hungry?" he asked Ellie.

Standing on his cushion in front of the bed, Blackjack barked once, signaling a yes.

"I wasn't talking to you, Your Majesty," Wyler said to Blackjack as he stretched. "But message received. How about you?"

Ellie sat up, the sheet draped over her chest. She woke her phone, checking the time.

"I could eat."

Wyler pulled on a pair of form-fitting boxers and left the room with Blackjack at his heels. He walked through his minimally furnished living room, consisting of a couch, a coffee table stacked with poker books, and a flat-screen TV. Clean, minimal, and devoid of distractions. Just the way he liked it. His peaceful oasis from a chaotic world.

He opened a window in the kitchen to let out some of the stale air. Then he got to preparing dinner. When it came to cooking, Wyler strove for simplicity. After setting a pot of rice to a simmer, he began slicing chunks of fresh tuna. Halfway through, Ellie's bare breasts pressed against his back. Her arms carefully slipped under his so as not to disrupt his cutting. She kissed a spot in the middle of his shoulder blades. Her skin was warm against his.

"Do I have time to hop in the shower?" she asked.

Wyler glanced at the timer for the rice. "A short one."

"That's all I need."

She kissed him again, uncoiled her grasp, and disappeared into the bathroom.

When the rice finished, Wyler compiled three bowls of rice, tuna, and cucumber. He gave Blackjack the first bowl and took the other two to the small table. Wyler sipped on a light beer while he waited for Ellie. She sat down fifteen minutes later, dressed and smelling fresh. Mascara and a high-sheen lip gloss were the only makeup she wore.

"This looks incredible," she said, picking up the metal chopsticks Wyler laid out for her. "When are you coming in tonight?"

"I'll go in with you. My buddy is coming around nine."

"Want me to save you two seats at a table?"

"Yeah, if you won't catch hell for it."

"Who's going to give me hell there?"

Wyler smiled. "I forgot who I was talking to."

Ellie smirked as she took a bite of food. When they finished eating, she asked, "Can I do the drill before we leave?"

"You brought the new batch. It's only right," Wyler said, collecting the empty bowls.

Ellie spun out of her chair and hurried to the hallway closet. Blackjack followed her with an equally enthusiastic trot. She pulled out a recyclable bag. Blackjack sniffed it as Ellie returned to the table. Blackjack dutifully sat in front of her. The first object she pulled from the bag was a set of rubber keys similar to what a toddler might play with.

"Keys," Ellie said to Blackjack, holding them in front of him. "Keys. Keys." She looked to Wyler in the kitchen. "How many times do I need to repeat it?"

"Put it back in the bag, then pull it out again. Say it two more times after that, then move on."

"Okay." Ellie did as instructed going through the remaining three items in the bag. When Ellie finished, she went into the living room and spread the four objects on the floor. Blackjack stayed in place until she returned.

"Okay, ready, Blackjack?" Ellie said. She waited until he focused on her. "Get the keys."

In an instant, Blackjack darted into the living room. He sniffed around the four objects. After thirty seconds of inspection, he snatched the keys into his mouth and brought them back. With a giddy little laugh, Ellie took the keys from Blackjack and patted him on the head.

"Correct. Good boy, Blackjack. Now, get the phone."

The dog followed the command for the next three objects, correctly choosing each one.

"He went four for four," Ellie said to Wyler.

"I think he's showing off for you."

"I don't blame him."

"Mark them on the board," Wyler said, nodding to a chalkboard that ran from floor to ceiling against a protruding support beam. Ellie scooped the piece of chalk and added the four objects to the list, numbering each.

"What's he at?" Wyler called from the kitchen sink.

"Ninety-six," Ellie responded. "Almost in triple digits."

Wyler joined Ellie at the board.

"Proud of yourself, aren't you?" Wyler said.

She beamed. "I am. Thank you."

"Good. You should be." Then he kissed her, lingering a moment on her bottom lip. When they parted, he said, "Give me five minutes to change, then we'll walk you in."

Chapter 2

The trio left the apartment half an hour before Ellie's shift. They walked south until hitting the famed Atlantic City boardwalk. Ellie threaded her fingers between Wyler's as they strolled through the hum of bustling tourists. Walking hand in hand with her felt natural and easy. Relationships were always somewhat of a mystery to Wyler. He'd grown up in the city to parents heavily entrenched in the world of gambling, providing him with questionable role models. His mother was a casino dealer and superb card counter that was often brought into her husband's hustling schemes. When he saw his parents together, which wasn't that often, they seemed happy enough, he thought. Their conversations revolved around deep analysis of what sports team would cover the spread and what eccentric person showed up in the casino that day. His parents' primary focus was money and how to make it quickly and easily. Not the clichés in movies he'd seen or books he read of love or family. Cold, hard cash was the center of their world. Once he enlisted in the Marines, relationships remained an abstract concept. Sure, some of the older guys had families, but they kept that close to themselves, which was understandable when they dealt with death for a job.

Then, he met Enola Harjo at the Blackstone Dog Sanctuary in Virginia, run by his billionaire friend, Arlo Riggins. And his views on relationships changed. He knew love, real love, for the first time. Their romance was relatively short but left an indelible mark on him. When she broke things off, wanting space to focus on her work, Wyler built a wall around the hole left behind in his heart. He didn't think he'd know that feeling again, nor was he positive he deserved the right. When Ellie came around, things started slow. He'd known her for over a year working—if playing Texas Holdem for six hours a day could be considered a job—at the Whitmore Club. A month into Blackjack's recovery from his gunshot wound, he had asked Ellie to watch the dog while he took care of an incident with his mom at the facility treating her Alzheimer's. Blackjack took to Ellie, and so did Wyler. And before he knew it, they were a thing.

The air was warm, and the sun cast a soothing orange haze across the city. The scene reminded Wyler of Norman Rockwell's work. In instances like this, he wished his life could be frozen in time like a painting, where there was no history or baggage, just the pleasantness of the moment.

The Whitmore Club occupied the first floor of a three-story building on the western end of the boardwalk. The facade had a worn appearance that harkened back to a bygone era during Prohibition when the streets were run by mob-connected mayor Nucky Johnson. The inside was a different story. Stylistic commissioned prints of poker legends like Doyle Brunson and Amarillo Slim hung on the exposed brick walls. The space was divided into three sections. Two were for poker and contained six ten-seat tables. The third room was dedicated to sports betting with wall-to-wall TVs. Identical bars stocked with premium liquors and craft beers rested against the side wall of each room. The Whitmore club attracted a gamut of player types, from pros and daily grinders to wannabes and tourists.

Wyler stood at the bar in the second poker room where Ellie worked. While waiting for Soto to arrive, he sipped a freshly poured Guinness. Blackjack, the one non-human patron allowed into the club, sat dutifully near Wyler's feet. Halfway through Wyler's pint, Soto entered the room. He wore navy slacks, tan loafers without socks and a purple and blue paisley button-down that was supposedly back in fashion for the Millennial crowd. The top three buttons of his shirt were undone, revealing a smooth, muscled chest. Soto's hair was trimmed short on the sides, with the top gelled into tiny spikes. Wyler noted the expensive watch that clung to Soto's wrist as he removed a thick pair of aviator sunglasses to scan the room. When Soto spotted Wyler, he grinned and held his arms out wide. Then he folded his sunglasses and hung them on his shirt. Soto navigated to the bar, where he shook Wyler's hand.

"Nice venue, brother," Soto said. He slapped his free hand on Wyler's bicep. "You look good."

"And you look thirsty. What can I get you?"

Wyler nodded at Ellie. She strolled over after disengaging from one of the regulars.

"Ellie, this is Tomás Soto," Wyler said. "He was a war grunt with me overseas back in the day. This is Ellie."

"How you doing?" she said.

Soto reached across the bartop to take Ellie's offered hand. He gently kissed her knuckles. Always one for theatrics.

"I'm better now," Soto said through a grin. His shame knew no bounds with the fairer sex. A flirtatious act that often got him into trouble.

"Oh, boy," Ellie laughed, rolling her eyes as she retracted her hand. "You're one of those guys, huh?"

"What kind of guy is that?" Soto said.

Ellie smirked but didn't answer. "What are you drinking?"

Soto squinted at the bottles behind her. He pointed at a small one shaped like a wine decanter with a light amber liquid inside.

"Is that Don Julio Real?"

Ellie followed his finger until she spotted the bottle. "It is."

"I'll have one of those. Neat with a splash of water."

"Okay," Ellie said. She looked at Wyler. "You all set?"

Wyler nodded. Ellie poured three fingers of tequila and a splash of Saratoga Spring water into a snifter. She placed the drink in front of Soto.

"There you go. First round's on the house," she said. "I'll leave you boys to it. If you need anything, give me a shout."

When Ellie was out of earshot, Soto grinned. "I see why you like it here."

"She's good people," Wyler said.

"I can imagine."

He hadn't changed a bit. For many, Soto was an acquired taste. Wyler found him to be entertaining more than anything. His zest for life was a mild drug that helped him escape the seriousness of the world for a brief moment. People couldn't help but be drawn to it.

"So, what brings you to my stomping grounds?" Wyler said.

Soto took a sip of the tequila, then sighed with appreciation. "I'm branching out. The L.A. market is getting a bit saturated with agents. Don't get me wrong; it's still my bread and butter. L.A. made me who I am today, but I'm looking to go to the next stage of my career. A lot of high-end buyers want multiple properties on each coast. It kills me to refer them to another agent. All I see is cash flying away."

"Why here?"

"A.C. has a lot of potential. I think it's undervalued at the moment. Obviously, New York is the crown jewel, but that's saturated, too. I'm trying to stake my claim on a location before it catches on. You know what I mean?"

"Sounds like you can be the next cast member on Million Dollar Listing."

"Oh, wow, look at you, Mr. Pop Culture."

"I've been called worse."

"I know." Soto smiled, looked down, and nearly spilled his drink when he noticed Blackjack. "Jesus, where'd he come from? Christ. He's been there this whole time?"

Wyler laughed. "You're losing a step."

"So you're still doing all that dog-whispering shit? This place doesn't mind him being in here?"

"I made an arrangement with the owner."

"Gotcha. Damn. How many clients do you have?"

"No clients. Just him."

"Really? If you could get everyone's dog acting like that, you'd be swimming in cash."

"Maybe." Wyler shrugged and sipped his beer.

"Is he friendly? Can I pet him?" Soto said, reaching out his hand.

"Depends if he thinks you're a threat or not."

"Serious?" Soto stopped his hand midway to Blackjack's head. Wyler took another swig of beer.

Soto stared at Blackjack, then laughed. He elbowed Wyler in the arm, realizing he was joking. "You're a son of bitch." He gave the dog a tentative scratch on the head. "Are we getting in a game or what?"

"That's why we're here."

"Then bottoms up, mother fucker." Soto raised his snifter. They clinked glasses. In one gulp, Soto drained the tequila. He exhaled forcefully as he set the glass on the bar top. "Let's make some money."

"Come on, I've got us a table over here."

Wyler navigated through the sea of green felt with Blackjack at his side and Soto bringing up the rear. They stopped by the large windows with a view of the nighttime ocean. Four people sat at the table. Three guys and a woman. The dealer, Charlotte, smiled as Wyler and Soto settled into two of the open chairs.

"Hey, Dec," the dealer said.

"Charlotte."

Wyler liked her as a dealer. She was fast and alert but also a true lover of the game. Charlotte was pushing forty, but her baby face made her look like someone in their late twenties. Wyler didn't personally know the other players at the table. He'd seen two of the guys before around the club but had yet to play them. They were in the midst of finishing a hand of Holdem. Two players remained invested in the pot. The hole cards got flipped over after a raise and a call on the river. The guy in the fifth position won the pot. As he raked in his chips, Wyler and Soto bought into the game with a grand apiece. Charlotte counted the cash and then stacked their chips.

The cards for the next hand spun onto the table. Wyler folded after the flop, and Soto followed suit after the turn. Wyler played conservatively the first half hour, getting a read on his opponents. After Soto won a hand and the tequila appeared to have kicked in, he grinned at Wyler. Then he tapped twice on the top of his chip stack. Wyler understood the signal from their war days. It meant that he was loose and ready to put on a show. Soto had a natural likeability and was an expert small talker, which lulled anyone he met into a sense of ease. He utilized these two attributes subtly yet effectively as part of his poker strategy. Soto rooted for the other players to win. He bought the table drinks. He tipped the dealer after every hand he collected. When Soto won, he played the part of a humble newcomer. These little factors collected over time to the point where he barely played the cards, but the people instead.

Wyler enjoyed the performance. He thought Soto had perfected his craft since the last time they'd played together. Being privy to Soto's tactics allowed Wyler to capitalize on the disarmed players. Once the table became enamored with Soto, Wyler did his best to disappear from his opponents' consciousness. He liked it that way. It made winning that much simpler.

At midnight, the table started to break up. One of the guys left, and the girl followed. The four of them played three more hands before the remaining two opponents cashed out their dwindled stacks in surrender. Soto stood and shook the player's hands with a parting remark that put a smile on their faces.

"Your routine's improved," Wyler said as Soto dropped into his chair.

Soto shrugged. "Years of practice will do that. Your game was tight, too. How'd you make out?"

Wyler studied his chips. "Doubled up. Not a bad night."

Soto waved his hand dismissively. "This is tip money, brother." He stood and tossed a generous number of chips to Charlotte.

"Thanks," she said. "You're welcome back anytime."

"I might take you up on that," he grinned. Soto nodded for Wyler to follow him. "Come on, let's ditch these chips, grab another drink, and talk."

Wyler led Soto to the cashier booth that was enclosed in cast iron slats. They exchanged their chips for crisp hundred-dollar bills, then returned to the bar. Ellie finished with a customer well on his way to a night he wouldn't remember.

"How'd you do?" she asked Wyler.

He flashed her the folded wad of bills. She raised her eyebrows, impressed.

"Looks like your friend should visit more often."

"That's the plan," Soto said. "I'll have the same as last time. This round's on me."

Ellie fixed the drinks, and Soto paid, leaving her a hundred-dollar tip. And the act continued. She looked at the bill, then at Wyler, who shrugged.

"You want change?" Ellie asked.

Soto shook his head, raising the glass. "It's yours."

Ellie smiled. "Okay."

As Soto stepped back from the bar, Wyler leaned in toward Ellie.

"Are you staying over tonight? I'll be here until you get off."

She collected an empty glass off the bar top. "Have fun with your friend. Don't worry about me."

"Who says I don't worry about you every night?"

Ellie smiled again. He wanted to kiss her, but he knew that was against protocol while she was working. For her tips to remain high, every man there needed to think she was available.

Wyler took his beer and found Soto by the windows.

"Let's sit outside," Soto said.

He pushed open the large glass doors that led onto a deck overlooking the ocean. Lights from the Atlantic City skyline flicked like neon stars against the night sky. Aside from two guys smoking, the space was devoid of people. They planted themselves at a table in the corner. Blackjack circled, then curled into a ball behind Wyler's chair. Waves breaking against the sand dulled the surrounding city sounds.

"It's good playing with you again, brother," Soto said. "Reminds me of that time we cleaned out those Army bums. You remember that?"

"When we were over in Kuwait."

"Yeah, man." Soto laughed. "You remember that one kid? He bet his grandfather's field knife from WWII. I don't think I've ever seen someone's face sink like his when I turned over those pocket cowboys."

"I doubt he ever gambled again after that."

"I should've kept that knife too. He was lucky I was in a good mood that day and gave it back to him."

"If I remember correctly, you sold it back to him."

Soto laughed again. "I mean, I couldn't walk away empty-handed. A bet's a bet. If I sold that knife today, I could buy a new car."

Wyler shook his head. "Always hustling."

Soto used his left hand to open his shirt, revealing a 'Always Hustling' tattoo on his chest. "I live and die by the motto, brother." He let the shirt fall closed. After sipping his tequila, he said, "I've got a job offer for you, a short job, an easy job for someone with your skills. Only take five days."

Here came the pitch, Wyler thought, waiting for the fastball to blow past home plate.

"This is the part where I ask, what kind of job?"

Soto shook his head. "I've got this friend, Ortega, Rafa Ortega, out in Vegas. We came up together in LA as real estate agents. Super smart, crushed it selling houses. Anyway, a few years ago, he moved out to Vegas to set up his own shop and transitioned over to the development side of real estate."

Wyler had no idea where this was going but remained silent while Soto continued.

"It's like the Wild West out there, and he's made…" Soto held his hand out flat and shook it slightly. "…some enemies. Anyway, as a side hustle, he breeds a few dogs, all above board, and he's looking to train some of them to be a part of his security detail."

The pitch turned into a curve ball and swung wide. Wyler nodded. "Uh-huh. And let me guess, you volunteered my name."

Soto sat forward, his eyes wide, almost manic. "And why shouldn't I? Few people can do what you can do to the level that you can do it. You're unique, Wyler. I witnessed firsthand what you can do with dogs. I mean, shit, look at this one." Soto aimed his hands at Blackjack like he was revealing a chest of gold. "And my man is willing to pay top dollar. A hundred grand. Fifty of it you'll get upfront, the other fifty when you finish. Easiest money you'll ever make."

"It's going to take longer than five days to get a dog trained like Blackjack," Wyler said.

Soto tapped Wyler on the arm with the back of his hand. "That's the best part. You don't have to train them the whole time. Think of it like a boot camp. You show Rafa's guys the basics and outline the blueprint of how to get the dogs to that level, and then they do all the hard work after that. You're a consultant. Even if the training doesn't stick, you still get paid." Soto leaned even closer, his words coming out rapidly. "Come on. Look me in the eyes and tell me this won't be the easiest money of your life."

Wyler conceded that it probably would be. And his current financial reserves had taken a hit during Blackjack's recovery period. During the first three months, he barely left Blackjack's side, which meant he wasn't gambling or pulling in security shifts at the casino. The money he got from Arlo from the Florida operation carried him for most of it. Still, after the repairs to his vehicle, medical expenses for Blackjack, and footing the bill for his mom's nursing home, he was stretched thin. A hundred grand for five days of work was a good deal, but Wyler had to consider the source. Soto wasn't known for his willingness to provide all the job details.

"And what do you get out of this?" Wyler said.

"Who says I get anything? Why can't this just be one friend helping another?"

Wyler smiled. "Shit, you can't even say that with a straight face."

Soto sat back, his lips spread in a sly grin. "Alright, fine. My friend said if you take the job and it pans out, as a finder's fee, he'll cut me in on his new development, giving me early access to his listings."

"There it is."

"What? There's no downside. We all win. Five days. Vegas. A hundred grand. We can even get in some gambling while you're out there, and you can make even more."

Wyler sipped on his beer as he studied Soto. Something felt off to him. Something in his friend's voice that almost felt...desperate.

"What aren't you telling me?" Wyler said.

Soto's face shifted, making it seem like Wyler had just insulted his mother. "Nothing. Jesus. Why would you say that?"

"Because you're 'always hustling,' remember?"

"This is your specialty," Soto said, his voice softening. "I thought you loved this shit. I thought you'd jump at the chance."

Wyler sighed. He wanted to take Soto's proposition at face value, but a sharp instinct in his gut made him weary.

"How about this," Soto said, leaning closer again. "Come out there and meet with Rafa. He plays cards, too. Let's get in a game, shoot the shit. You can feel him out. If, after talking to him, you don't want to do it, then you bail. And to sweeten the pot, I'll even pay for your hotel and flight, both ways. So you lose nothing in the process."

"I don't fly."

"What?"

Wyler nodded at Blackjack. "He comes with me. If I'm going, I drive."

Soto shook his head, slightly annoyed. "Okay. Fine, then I'll pay for your gas."

"I converted my Bronco to electric."

"Jesus, you're not making this easy," Soto sighed as he massaged his forehead. "Fine, I'll pay your electric bill for the month then, okay? Christ. Will you come then?"

"And when would this need to happen?"

"As soon as you can."

"Why the rush?"

"Rafa understands it will take some time, so the sooner the

training starts, the better." Soto paused, studying Wyler, clearly debating saying something else. He tapped his fingers against the snifter, drumming out a hollow-sounding beat. "I hate to have to do this, but I'm sensing some resistance here. You're forcing my hand, so I'm cashing my chip in. You know what I'm talking about?"

"I remember."

Six years ago, Wyler went home to Atlantic City after leaving the Marines. His father had been killed in prison when Wyler was twenty-four. He hadn't been back since the funeral. And what he returned to shocked his system. His mom was penniless and alone, still living in their childhood apartment. Worse, though, she barely recognized her own son. It wasn't until five months later that she was diagnosed with an aggressive case of Alzheimer's disease. At first, he took care of her, but then it became too much. They had been living off of his military savings, which vanished almost instantly after getting her admitted to a private care facility. He could've put her somewhere State-run, but she was the only family he had left, and he wanted her to have the best treatment for however long she had left.

At that point, Wyler turned to a skill he knew best—gambling. He had success early on but was undisciplined in managing his bankroll. Playing for petty cash and smokes in the Marines vastly differed from playing to pay the bills. After an extended run of bad beats at the tables, Wyler couldn't pay the rent or his mother's facility fees. Soto was the one who bailed him out. As an up-and-coming real estate agent, he was flush with cash and made a deal with the landlord not to evict Wyler. On top of that, he paid his mom's facility costs for three months until Wyler landed back on his feet.

"I helped you out, didn't I?" Soto said.

"Yes."

"Don't get me wrong, I was glad to help. And I didn't ask for anything in return?"

Wyler nodded. "But you are now."

"That's right."

Wyler stared at the neon lights in the distance while he processed the risks versus the rewards of what Soto wasn't telling him. At his present calculation, the risks of the unknown were hovering in the sixty percent range. None of which mattered, though. His marker had been called, and unlike his father, Wyler paid his debts.

"I do this and we're square?" Wyler asked.

"We'll never talk about it again."

Wyler sighed. "If your man can double it to two hundred grand, I'm in. I can leave tomorrow and be out there in about six days."

Soto grinned as he stood up, pulling his phone from his pocket. "I knew you'd say yes. Let me call my boy to confirm the price. Hold tight."

Soto walked out of earshot. His phone call lasted less than thirty seconds. When Soto returned, the corners of his grin reached for the back of his head.

"Pack your bags," he said. "We're going to Vegas."

Chapter 3

A day later, Wyler got out of bed at ten. After he and Blackjack completed a two-mile jog, Wyler showered and dressed. While eating breakfast, he plotted the drive to Vegas on his laptop. The map calculated the two thousand five hundred-mile trip would take roughly thirty-seven hours. To make it to Vegas in six days, he would have to drive at least six hours daily. He considered that more than manageable. With the route set, he next marked out all his stop point locations. Feeling confident in his travel plans, Wyler packed for the trip, sticking to the essentials to keep his load light.

Vegas to Wyler was almost like a second home. It shared a similar DNA to Atlantic City but without the ocean and hotter temperatures. Like most locales built around gambling, people arrived with dreams of fortune and glory. They put their hopes of a better life on the toss of a dice or the spin of a roulette wheel.

Many left with their dreams shattered, boarding their planes and heading home covered in disillusionment. Ecstasy and ruin were in constant battle in places like Vegas and Atlantic City. It was in this type of environment where Wyler grew up and was most at ease.

In the spare bedroom, Wyler opened one of his two industrial cabinets. From a safe bolted to the top shelf, he counted out five grand in hundred dollar bills, a thousand of which he separated into two piles of five hundred that he folded into palm-sized squares and tucked into each of his socks. It was a safety precaution learned from his dad. "People might check your shoes," his dad had said, "but who's going to check your socks? No one. Well, some might, but only the smart ones and most of these chumps around here rely on their muscles, not their brains, like us. These guys see dirty, sweaty socks...they don't want to deal with that. What do I always tell you? Play the odds. Odds are, the guys in our world aren't checking your socks."

When Wyler was fifteen, he saw the advice put to the test up close and personal. It was after Wyler's dad had been on a particularly rough losing streak. A loan shark, the size of an actual great white shark, cornered them in the bathroom of a movie theater. They had just finished watching Quentin Tarantino's *Kill Bill*. Wyler was in mid-sentence reminiscing about the epic ending fight scene when the loan shark appeared. He gripped Wyler's dad's neck with fingers as hard-looking as pliers. Through a harsh, raspy voice, the loan shark asked for his money. He made his dad turn out all his pockets, empty his wallet, and remove his shoes. After inspecting each area and seeing no cash, the loan shark expressed his displeasure and a new payment timeline attached with unsubtle threats of physical harm. Once the loan shark was gone, Wyler's dad sat on the toilet. Unphased, he pulled out a fold of money from his sock.

"No one checks the socks," he said with a grin. Wyler forced a smile despite being scared shitless. That day, he gained a new respect for actual violence.

Coming out of the memory, Wyler took the remaining four grand and folded it in with his winnings from the other night with Soto. He stuck to the most basic gambling rule he learned the hard way: don't play with what you can't afford to lose. He never took credit cards and quit when the cash was gone. Strictly adhering to the discipline had allowed him to come back from his earlier mistakes and continue to live the life of a poker player.

The last item he took was his pair of custom-made tungsten carbide knuckledusters. They were a weapon mired in state-to-state regulations ranging from partial bans to outright illegality, as in New Jersey and Nevada. They were a risk to carry, but if he needed to ditch them, it was far cheaper and generally safer than leaving a firearm behind. He didn't anticipate needing them but liked having the option if the occasion arose.

By one o'clock, Wyler was ready to go. He went into the bedroom with Blackjack by his side. Wyler sat on the edge of the bed and pushed a lock of hair from Ellie's face.

"Leaving already?" she said through a sleepy frown.

"I want to put some miles behind us today. Keys are on the table. Come and go as you please."

"Alright. Call me when you get there, yeah?"

"I will."

"When will you be back?"

"Six-day drive, then five days of work, then six days back. So, seventeen days." Wyler smiled. "Think you'll be able to survive that long without me?"

Ellie returned the smile. "It'll be tough, but I'm sure I can summon the intestinal fortitude to do it." She propped up on her elbow. "Does this job mean we'll be able to take that vacation together?"

"It does."

"Any more thoughts on where you'd want to go?"

"Wherever you are is a vacation for me."

Ellie laughed as she dropped her head back to the pillow. "Oh, please. That's a new one I'll have to file in the cornball folder."

Wyler grinned. "I'll think about it on the drive. I'll have plenty of time."

"That you will."

Wyler leaned in and kissed her. Ellie's lips lingered on his for a long breath. When she parted, she whispered. "Be safe."

"Always."

She looked at Blackjack then. "Well, are you going to say goodbye or what?"

Blackjack barked once. He put his front paws on the edge of the bed and licked Ellie on the cheek.

"Try not to miss me too much," Ellie said, scratching Blackjack's scruff. "Make sure you watch out for him."

Wyler whistled, and Blackjack followed him out of the room. He grabbed their gear, put the collar on Blackjack, and they were out the door.

A block to the east, Wyler and Blackjack arrived at a three-floor parking garage. On the second floor, along the inside wall, rested a 1978 Ford Bronco with a rust-colored exterior. Aside from Blackjack, the Bronco was Wyler's pride and joy. He converted the vehicle to electric power and updated the interior with modern technology. The back seat was replaced with a solid floor as a place for him and Blackjack to sleep. Wyler ran his hand over the recently refreshed paint job after it had sustained several bullet holes from his operation in Florida. It cost him extra to pay the mechanics to not ask questions. They had done fine work, Wyler thought.

He opened the back and stored their gear in a compartment under the floor. Once Blackjack was seated, Wyler turned the key, and the Bronco sparked to life. With the destination set in the center console GPS, he shifted into drive, ready for the city of sin.

Six days and two thousand five hundred and thirty-five miles later, Wyler and Blackjack arrived in Las Vegas. After camping in the Bronco the night before outside Salt Lake City, Wyler drove the remaining five hours straight through. It was a Friday night, and the city bustled with activity. In desperate need of a shower, Wyler headed for the hotel Soto had booked for him. He pulled into the parking lot of the JW Marriott in Sumerlin. It had the sprawling grandeur of what Wyler imagined a ritzy old-world European casino resort would look like. Palm trees lined the path of the regal entrance. He pulled up to the front, where an attentive valet hustled over.

"Hello, sir," the valet said as Wyler got out. "Do you need assistance with your bags?"

"No. I'm good. Thanks," Wyler responded, stepping back so Blackjack could hop down.

"Oh," the valet said, stopping short. "I wasn't expecting him."

"Most people aren't."

A nervous smile spread across the valet's face as he tore off the return ticket and handed it to Wyler. In exchange, Wyler passed him a folded twenty-dollar bill.

"If you could park it away from other cars, I'd appreciate it."

The valet tucked the money into his pocket without checking the denomination and said, "Can do."

Wyler grabbed his gear from the trunk, and he and Blackjack strolled into the hotel lobby. A middle-aged woman sat behind the reception desk with a name badge adorning her crisply pressed beige blazer. Dawn. The name fit her pleasantly attentive face. She flashed a thin-lipped smile when her eyes caught Wyler's. It quickly vanished when she noticed Blackjack.

"I'm sorry, sir," she said. "We don't allow pets in here."

"I understand, but I was told an exception had been made."

She paused and squinted at him. He almost thought she might call for security.

"An exception?" She continued to study his face, debating how she wanted to continue. "What is your name?"

"Declan Wyler."

She shifted her suspicious gaze to the computer to her left and began typing. After a few clicks of the mouse, her face softened.

"Oh, yes. I see that in the notes here. Please accept my apologies, I—"

"Don't even mention it."

After a few more apologies, she handed over the keycard to his room and gave him directions to the elevators. They exited on the fourth floor. Wyler navigated to the place that would serve as his home for the next five days. It was larger than he anticipated. A king-size bed jutted out from the left wall. In the center stood a varnished floor-to-ceiling TV stand that separated a living space, complete with a couch, coffee table, and two plush guest chairs. At the back wall was a glass double door leading to a patio. Wyler opened it, and Blackjack followed him out. A panoramic view of the jagged mountain landscape stretched as far as the eye could see. Insects softly chirping provided a natural symphony.

"Looks like we're getting a taste of high society," Wyler said to Blackjack.

The dog barked once and wagged his tail as he watched a large hawk lazily drift through the sky.

"Yeah, well, don't get used to it. We have to go home eventually."

Soto had spared no expense, which meant he really needed Wyler to accept the job. Wyler went back to their conversation in Atlantic City. Soto said he'd get more listings. So, was this purely a money play? Something about that didn't sit right with Wyler, though. If Soto was expanding his territory to the East Coast, it would imply he was doing well financially. So why would it be vital for him to get the listings from Ortega? And if Ortega was his supposed friend, wouldn't he just give him the listings anyway? Why make it contingent upon him training a couple of dogs? Wyler stopped himself from analyzing too deeply into Soto's motivations. He was there now and saw no immediate dangers in meeting with Ortega.

Wyler's phone buzzed. He answered.

"What do you think of the room?" Soto said.

"It's big. How'd you know I was here?"

"I sold the hotel owner's daughter a place in Santa Monica a few years ago. Got her a steal for it. He does me some favors now and again at the hotel as a show of appreciation. I asked him to notify me when you arrived."

"Seems like a wasted favor to me."

"Getting your dog in there was the favor, brother," Soto laughed. "Anyway, my boy Rafa is down to meet with you tonight at his house. You game? Or do you need a day?"

"You already committed to tonight, didn't you?"

"I could reschedule if you need your rest, old man."

Wyler sighed and checked his watch. It was seven o'clock. "What time?"

"Nine-thirty. He said we could play some cards first as a little icebreaker. Then we can get down to the details of the job."

"Alright. I can make that work."

"My man. I'll be over in an hour to pick you up. We can have a drink before we go. He lives close to the hotel."

"Roger that."

"Peace, brother."

After Wyler showered, he got dressed in a pair of slim-fit khakis, white low-top sneakers, and a Carolina blue short-sleeved button-down shirt dotted with a pattern of tiny white palm trees. Polished casual was how he liked to describe his style. He found it worked for most occasions and felt confident it wouldn't offend Soto's wealthy friends. Wyler then called Ellie to let her know he had arrived safely. When he hung up, he grabbed a dog brush, went onto the balcony with Blackjack, and began to brush him. At ten past eight, there was a knock on the door.

Soto stood in the hallway holding a six-pack of beer. Two bottles were already missing.

"How was the drive?" Soto said, spilling into the room. A scent of liquor radiated from him. His forehead glistened with sweat. Red streaks spiderwebbed in his eyes. He looked as though he'd been on a three-day bender. Wyler didn't like to entangle himself in what people did to themselves. He witnessed the worst in humanity during his eight years in war-torn regions. So had Soto.

How people coped with those realities wasn't for him to judge.

"You good?" Wyler asked.

"You're crazy doing that drive," Soto said, cutting through the room to the balcony. "I'd go nuts. I'll take a plane any chance I can get. Anything over an hour, and I'm flying. Ready for a cold one?"

Wyler declined, not wanting to further encourage Soto down whatever hole he was falling. The signs he exhibited put an uneasy tension in Wyler's gut, but he let it slide for the time being. Soto set the six-pack on a small table flanked by two chairs, grabbed a bottle, twisted the cap off, and chucked it into the darkening distance. Wyler sat in one of the chairs and resumed brushing Blackjack's thick coat. Soto quietly drank his beer while he gazed at the sun-bleached earth. Then he said, "This heat and landscape reminds me of Iraq."

"Not far off."

Soto pointed with his beer bottle at Blackjack. "Do you ever think about the people you saved over there? You and your dogs?"

The question caught Wyler off guard. "How much did you drink before you came over here?"

"Just a splash of something," Soto said, pinching his thumb and index finger together.

"Sounds like more than a splash."

Soto waved him off. "Do you?"

"Honestly?"

"Yeah. I mean, I helped some guys out, but just in the way of doing the day-to-day stuff. You know? Just part of doing the job. You, though, you and the dog, were a specialized weapon. If you guys weren't there, who knows how many more of us would be dead."

Wyler set the brush down and swept his hands over Blackjack

until the loose hair vanished.

"I wish that's how it was," Wyler said. "If I think about my time over there, I usually think about the ones I didn't save. Those ones usually form a clearer picture."

"Really?"

Wyler shrugged, then relocated to the rail next to his friend. "You sweep a road and clear it of a couple IEDs. The humvees just roll past. You carry on. Like you said, the day-to-day stuff, no one's throwing you a party." He stared into the distance with Soto, almost able to picture humvees rolling across the earth and hear the gravel crunching beneath massive tires. "But when some kid's laying in the dirt missing his leg, bleeding out from a bomb you missed...I don't know...guess that sticks with you longer. It's easy to quantify those. But people saved, that's like asking you if you remember all the people you've held a door open for. It's more abstract."

Soto nodded. His eyes took on a glassy, far-off look.

"I think...I think about the people that died next to me...the ones I let down...the ones I couldn't save," Soto said. "I see some of their faces sometimes. That ever happen to you?"

Wyler studied Soto. "Sometimes." They were quiet for a beat. Then Wyler asked, "Are you alright?"

Soto broke his trance on the landscape. He took another pull on the beer, then laughed. But it was filled with more sadness than mirth. "Listen to me. Get me in the desert, and I start dredging up old shit. Ignore me, huh?" Soto chugged the remainder of his beer, then checked his watch. "We should get going."

As they returned to the room, Wyler stepped in front of Soto. "You can talk to me, you know."

"That's what I'm doing, isn't it?" Soto shifted his focus to the ground as if he were suddenly embarrassed by revealing a part of himself. "I'm fine. Just had one drink too many. Forget about anything I said tonight, okay?"

Wyler wasn't buying it. He pressed Soto gently. "Anything you're not telling me?"

Soto's eyes darted to Wyler's, then away again. "Like what?" He laughed again, this time with a nervous undertone. "No. Nothing, brother. We're good. This is good. You're going to like Rafa. I promise. It's going to be easy money."

Wyler searched Soto's face for any discernible tells. He was positive Soto was holding something back, but he couldn't grasp what it was. Wyler pushed his reservations aside as thoughts of the potential payday came to mind. Two hundred grand, he told himself. Forty grand a day.

Wyler shrugged. "If you say you're good, then you're good."

"That's right," Soto said. "Trust me, brother, everything's going to be fine."

Chapter 4

The valet jumped out of a gleaming black Range Rover, leaving the driver's side door open for Soto. Wyler let Blackjack into the backseat, then climbed in front next to Soto.

"Nice ride," Wyler said.

"When I'm out here, I rent only the best."

Soto shifted into drive, then eased away from the hotel entrance. As he pulled onto the main road, lights from sprawling mansions dotted the night landscape.

"A lot of new money out in this region," Soto said. "Celebrities and tech tycoons have been moving here recently for the tax breaks. California's too expensive and driving them out of there. Vegas is a growing market that's only going to get bigger."

"And you're going to be able to handle all these different regions?"

"As one area does well, I can start building a team of my own.

Then, eventually, I'll just be able to sit back and rake in the money."

"That's the dream?"

"That's the dream, brother."

Soto turned down another residential street with more big boxy homes. The Range Rover drove toward the mountains, their jagged outline just visible under the moon's light. The road ended in a cul-de-sac. Soto stopped at a massive metal gate, flanked by stucco walls that rose ten feet high on either side. It had the vibe of an upscale fortress. Wyler couldn't tell how far the walls went in the dim light. Soto rolled down his window and spoke into a flat-screen monitor about the size of an iPad.

"Names," a clear voice said from the device.

"Tomás Soto, and Declan Wyler."

After a five-second pause, the voice said, "Come on up." Then, the gate silently slid into a recess in the stucco wall.

"You sure this guy isn't Saudi royalty?" Wyler said, impressed as he gaped at the sprawling estate. "It's quite the setup."

"He takes his security seriously," Soto said, driving past the gate. "That's why you're here, remember?"

Wyler nodded and looked out the window. Light poles lit the road that cut through the desert. Cameras affixed to them tracked their progress. He didn't take real estate developers for being the cutthroat types that would require such extensive defenses. Brutal dictators, sure. But guys in suits, haggling over empty chunks of land. Didn't make sense, but then again, most things wealthy people did didn't make sense to him.

Soto drove slowly for at least another quarter mile. In total, Wyler estimated they were roughly five miles from his hotel. The street leveled off, and the house came into view. It was two stories tall with a smooth white exterior and matching stone columns.

Six windows stretching from floor to ceiling lined the front face. The architecture carried a sleek modernity that complemented its surroundings.

"Damn," Wyler said. "Place must have cost, what, ten million?"

Soto didn't answer. He gripped the steering wheel with enough pressure to snap it in two.

"What?" Soto said, glancing at Wyler and then away.

"Nevermind."

From the lights radiating off the house, Wyler noticed a bead of sweat running down the side of Soto's face despite the air conditioning blasting. His demeanor unsettled Wyler. Whatever Soto wasn't telling him, he had a feeling was about to come out. The place looked normal enough, nonthreatening, but that didn't mean anything. Ted Bundy was nonthreatening on the outside, too. Wyler shook off his reservations and thought of his possible payday. Two hundred grand, he reminded himself—two hundred grand for five days of work and then your debt is square.

Soto parked in the wide driveway in front of a five-car garage. He killed the engine and sat there a second, staring straight ahead. Then he blinked like a camera shutter. The snap of which shook him from his daze. He opened his door and got out. Wyler and Blackjack followed after him to the house entrance. Soto ran his fingers through his hair and wiped the perspiration from his face with the back of his wrist. He stopped a foot from the door and faced Wyler. His eyes were wild with fear and desperation. He spoke quickly.

"Listen, if Rafa says anything different than what I told you about the job, just roll with it, yeah?"

The sound of alarm bells ricocheted through Wyler's skull like a frantic bird trying to escape its cage. "Wait. What?—" Before he could ask a follow up question, the door swung open.

A man, about five-eight, stood there wearing an unbuttoned black lightweight jacket that covered a blank silver t-shirt. Dark gray jeans with plain leather cowboy boots completed the look. His skin was a smooth, warm brown. Mexican, Wyler guessed. Maybe in his late thirties. Wild black hair matched equally wild eyes. They burned with an intensity that could start a forest fire.

"What's up, Tenoch?" Soto said, switching the charm act back on.

Tenoch's head shifted slightly so his flame thrower eyes were aimed at Soto. He nodded, then swung the twin flames back to Wyler, who didn't look away.

"Lift up your arms," Tenoch said. His voice was low and gravelly, like he'd spent a lifetime barking orders.

"What?" Soto said.

"Lift up your arms so I can search you for weapons," Tenoch said.

"Shit, man, we don't have any weapons."

Tenoch silenced Soto with another fiery glare. Soto sighed, then raised his arms. Tenoch worked quickly, patting down Soto's body. Wyler thought this wasn't the first time the man had done this. He was thorough, alert, and hit all the places Wyler would have checked. When he finished, he stepped toward Wyler.

"You too," he said.

Wyler obliged the command, and the hands worked over his body. They stopped at his pants pockets, patting them twice before diving in without asking Wyler's permission. He pulled out the knuckledusters and stepped back.

"What do you call these?" Tenoch said.

Based on his reaction, the discovery was about to go one of two ways: bad or catastrophic. Taking the knuckledusters with him was second nature to Wyler. It was like taking car keys. Easy to forget they were even there. But he hadn't anticipated being searched. Based on the two expanding balls of fire in Tenoch's eyes and the blood draining from Soto's face, Wyler guessed the next few seconds were headed for catastrophic.

"That's not...those aren't...weapons," Soto whispered.

"I wasn't talking to you."

"They're custom-made titanium knuckledusters," Wyler said. "Most people call them brass knuckles, but since they aren't made of brass, I don't like calling them that."

"No weapons," Tenoch said.

"Based on the bulge at your hip, I'd say you're armed with something a little more powerful," Wyler said, nodding at Tenoch's waist. "If you're scared of two pieces of metal, though, you can hold on to them."

A grin spread across Tenoch's face, making Stephen King's Pennywise look like a character from *Sesame Street*. Wyler had come across hard men before. Jihadists that wouldn't blink twice at beheading a child. Generals willing to sacrifice thousands of lives to protect an oil refinery. Dictators allowing millions of their citizens to starve. Wyler got the impression Tenoch would be right at home amongst those types of men.

"You're a brave man, Mr. Wyler," Tenoch said, stepping closer. "Maybe we should see how brave—"

"That's enough," a voice said from inside the house. A man in a casual white suit with no tie and brown high polished wing tips walked towards them. He carried a drink in one hand, and placed the other on Tenoch's shoulder.

"Mr. Wyler is our guest. Let's not offend him so quickly." The man smiled and held out his free hand to Wyler. "Rafa Ortega.

Thank you for coming."

Wyler shook Rafa's hand and studied the thin, clean-shaved face. A quarter-inch section of Rafa's right eyebrow was missing. And the eye below it had a slightly opaque sheet over it as if it had suffered damage at some point. When Rafa turned to nod a greeting to Soto, Wyler noticed the unique structure of his right ear. The top half of it was missing. The edge wasn't clean, indicating to Wyler its removal wasn't done by a sharp object. Torn off instead of sliced. He guessed it was probably from a long time ago based on the coloration and hardened skin.

"Fine craftsmanship," Rafa said, taking the knuckledusters from Tenoch. "I'm sure they leave a nasty mark." He offered them on the palm of his hand back to Wyler. "Accept my apologies. Tenoch has looked out for me since we were kids. If it wasn't for him, this..." Rafa tapped his mangled ear with his index finger. "... would've been a lot worse."

"An animal?" Wyler said, returning the knuckledusters to his pockets.

"Yes. A dog, actually. Speaking of which, who is this?" Rafa said, motioning to Blackjack with his drink.

"Blackjack," Wyler said.

"Well, I'm glad you brought an example of what you can do. Soto has filled me in on some of your exploits. Very impressive." Rafa waved and turned. "Please, come in. Would you care for a drink?"

"I'm good," Wyler said.

Tenoch's eyes burned a hole through Wyler as he brushed past him.

"How about you?" Rafa said to Soto.

"Sure. Whatever you're having," he said. The color returned

to his face as he forced a reassuring smile at Wyler.

Rafa passed two minimally decorated rooms with a sophisti-cated desert aesthetic. When Wyler thought of Western homes, he pictured antlers over fireplaces and Native American blankets hung on walls with ancient artifacts littering coffee tables. Wyler spotted some of those elements, but they had been converted into stylized monochromatic works of art that could've been pulled from the MoMA in New York. The home had an eerie bare silence to it. It was how Wyler imagined the interior of a manned rocket might sound drifting through the cosmos.

"Is this your first time in Las Vegas?" Rafa asked as they walked.

"No."

"Where are you staying?"

"I put him up in the JW Marriott down the road from here," Soto answered.

Rafa nodded. "Good. That would've been my choice. Very classy."

The floor plan opened into a vast, airy section at the end of the hallway. A matte black dinner table rested in front of a glass wall leading out to a lighted patio. Sitting at the table were two more men. Both Mexican, both equally as dangerous looking as Tenoch. They were on the shorter side but with lean physiques. They wore matching black t-shirts and had similar buzzed haircuts. At first glance, Wyler mistook them for twins. The only distinguishing feature was their tattoos. The guy on the right had what looked like a scorpion tattoo curling from his collarbone up around his neck, with the pointed tail stopping just below his left ear. The guy on the left had a snake tattoo, almost like a noose, coiled around his throat. Neither man spoke, nor did Rafa or Tenoch offer any introductions.

To the right was a wide marble-topped island that divided an expansive kitchen, which gleamed with stainless steel appliances, likely costing somewhere in the six-figure region. Rafa set his drink on the island and went to a section lined with liquor bottles.

"So, you drove here all the way from New Jersey?" Rafa said over his shoulder as he grabbed a glass from a cabinet.

"That's right," Wyler said, making notes of the exits. He found an uneasiness creeping into his stomach.

"You grew up out there, right?"

"Born and raised."

Rafa finished fixing Soto's drink and walked to the island. "You served eight years in the Marines. Did three tours in Afghanistan and Iraq. Were a highly decorated soldier in the dog handling program. No easy feat to get into, from my understanding." Rafa set the glass in front of Soto, then continued. "Honorable discharge at age twenty-eight. Helped establish cutting-edge programs at the Blackstone Sanctuary in Virginia with your friend, Arlo Riggins."

"I sound pretty impressive when you lay out my resume like that," Wyler said, grinning, trying to cut some of the tension after the pat down. He understood the tactic Rafa was deploying. It effectively exerted control over a situation by showing the person how much they knew about you. It didn't bother Wyler. As a poker player, he was used to being analyzed regularly.

"That you do," Rafa said, smiling back. "Knowing about the people I'm trying to do business with is helpful. Saves me time in the long run."

"I didn't know land development was such a dangerous profession."

Rafa shrugged. "When it comes to money, lots of money, anything can become a dangerous profession."

"I guess that's true."

"No. There's no guesswork in that statement. Just reality."

Wyler nodded. "Well, you've got me out here. How can I help make your world less dangerous?"

Rafa chuckled. "Direct. No wasting time. I like that. I thought we might play some cards first."

Wyler didn't want to be rude, but something was off and he didn't want to stick around any longer than he needed to. He didn't know why but the lack of ambient noise was getting to him. The house felt clinical like he was being observed by men in white coats behind a two-way mirror.

"Another time maybe," Wyler said. "I've been driving for days and am looking forward to catching up on some rest in a regular bed."

"Understandable," Rafa said, nodding politely. He came around the island, holding his hand out toward the glass wall. "If we're going to get right to it then, it'll be easier if I show you."

"Alright."

The twins got up from the table and opened the glass doors. Rafa led the way onto the white stone patio. A blissful wave of subtle sounds returned. The whoosh of air and the hum of electricity powering the filter of an elegant pool, calmed some of Wyler's growing anxiety. The backyard was boxed in by a wall similar to the one at the entrance to the estate. Soto downed his drink in one shot. He eased off his chair and stiffly walked with the look of a man on death row. Tenoch hung to the rear. Wyler didn't enjoy having him out of his direct line of sight, but there wasn't much he could do about it. Once the group exited the house, the twins plucked flashlights off their belts and headed for the wall.

"Follow me," Rafa said.

The Scorpion-tattooed man ran his fingers over a spot on the surface, stopped, and pressed. A section hissed, then began to move. The twins disappeared through the newly formed doorway, and then Rafa went after them.

"Where are we going?" Wyler asked as he stepped through to the other side.

"You'll see," Rafa said, walking beside Wyler. "I grew up in Los Angeles but my father lived a different life in Mexico. I would spend summers with him. He was a businessman of sorts. And one of the lessons he taught me was that some parts of ourselves are better kept hidden from the outside world."

The twins swept their flashlights over the dry earth as the terrain pitched downwards.

"And what type of business was your father in?" Wyler said. He glanced over his shoulder to locate Tenoch. He couldn't spot him amongst the shadows, but he knew he was there like a spectral being. Soto quietly moved along. Much like the house, his silence unnerved Wyler. What was he holding back? Wyler didn't enjoy not being able to see the bigger picture.

"He was in manufacturing and exports," Rafa said. "He also enjoyed gambling. And from my sources, I'm told your parents did too."

"Yeah. My mom was a blackjack dealer for a long time. She was good at counting cards. Really good if I'm being honest. And my dad... let's just say he lived for it. Anything and everything he would bet on. I don't think a day went by that he didn't bet on something."

"It must have been an interesting childhood."

"That's one way of putting it."

"It couldn't have been that bad if you followed in their footsteps after your time in the service anyway," Rafa said. He sighed then. "Some people hate what their parents do, how they are, who they are, and they try to go the opposite direction when they grow up. Not you, though."

"There were times I bucked against it. That's what I thought joining the Marines was.... I thought it would show them I wasn't like them...that I was somehow above their lifestyle choices."

"But you came back to it?"

"After eight years of a structured life doing other people's bidding for causes that didn't make much sense...yeah...I started to see the appeal of charting my own path without answering to anyone. I saw maybe they were on to something after all."

Rafa responded with a contemplative, *hmm*.

"Real estate sounds pretty different from manufacturing," Wyler said. "So you went the opposite direction from your father?"

"Yes and no. I went a little of both ways as well, I suppose."

They were about two hundred yards from the house when the twins paused. A ramp cut through the earth, about the width of two men. Solar-powered lighting apparatuses embedded into the dirt walls cast the path in a soft, fiery glow.

"It's not much farther now," Rafa said.

Wyler had no idea where the hell they were taking him. He started feeling like he was about to be initiated into some ancient cult. Soto remained silent behind him. And he still couldn't spot Tenoch. The risks were rapidly outbalancing the rewards Wyler had initially calculated. Two hundred grand was beginning to feel substantially low.

The twins went first, then Rafa. Wyler caught Soto's eyes and squinted as if to say, *what have you got me involved with?* Soto didn't say anything. He nodded for Wyler to keep going. Blackjack brushed against Wyler's leg as they descended the ramp until the walls reached two feet above his head. After twenty feet, the path fed into a crudely dug-out section, roughly the size of a large bathroom. A net served as the ceiling of the space. It swayed against the breeze in gentle waves. Directly in front of Wyler, Rafa stood by a massive metal door that looked like it could barricade the pathway to the underworld.

Rafa swiped a card across a box embedded into the earth. After it beeped, Rafe gripped the bar that curved out from the door and said, "We're here."

Motion-sensor lights flicked to life as Wyler passed the threshold. They led down a corridor reminiscent of freshly built Parisian catacombs. Cool air surrounded Wyler, and he surprisingly didn't smell any dampness.

"What is this place?" Wyler said.

"Welcome to the anillo de guerra," Rafa said. "Or the ring of war."

"Dramatic name."

Rafa grinned. "True. But it's fitting. We finished construction two years ago. The outer support structure was made from shipping containers, and the stonework was built afterward. It's completely powered by solar energy with geothermal heating and cooling systems connected to a network of duct systems to circulate the air. It was designed carefully to be as self-sufficient as possible."

"Guess you're all set for the end of the world," Wyler said in an attempt to hide the tension steadily pressing against his chest.

"It could serve that purpose if needed," Rafa said. "But right now, it's used to generate a tertiary income stream. This will be your new office." The path split left and right at the end of the thirty-foot corridor. "I'll give you the lay of the land."

The twins went left, triggering more automatic lights. The corridor stretched fifteen feet before breaking right at a ninety-degree angle. As Wyler followed, he glanced over his shoulder again. This time, he spotted Tenoch trailing a few feet behind Soto. It didn't put his mind at ease, but he felt better knowing where the man was. Up ahead, the twins were in the process of opening another heavy gunmetal gray door. As they approached, Wyler noticed Blackjack slow his pace and stiffen. The hair on his shoulders raised as he released a low growl. Wyler recognized the signs that whatever lay beyond the door wasn't anything good.

Chapter 5

The noise was the first thing that hit Wyler. Barking. Lots of dogs barking. The second thing to hit him was the smell. A mix of dander and piss, cut by an undercurrent of bleach. Circular overhead lights were already on inside the new room. It was big and square, at least thirty feet by thirty feet. Ten cages, each containing a dog except for two of them, lined the left wall. Crates filled with food flanked an identical metal door along the back wall. The right side of the room was divided into three sections by chest-high partitions, like a horse stable.

"This is where life begins," Rafa shouted over the increasing volume. "The breeding room."

He sauntered forward with one hand in his pocket and the other motioning to the first stall on the right. It was set up with an operating table and movable light. Harnesses dangled from the ceiling. Behind the table was a glass cabinet filled with various medical supplies.

"We have a licensed veterinarian as part of the staff that oversees any injuries and necessary surgeries," Rafa said. He moved casually as if Wyler were a prospect looking to buy a house. Blackjack paced anxiously at Wyler's side. The noise was overwhelming for Wyler. He could only imagine what it was doing to Blackjack.

"Easy," Wyler said to him and scratched Blackjack's head.

Rafa continued to the next stall, which had more harnesses lower to the ground and a contraption that looked like a stockade. "And here's where conception takes place. Sometimes, it's through natural methods. Other times...well...we take the more scientific route." He stopped at the last stall, which had a sizeable plush dog bed against the back wall, shelves of canned formula, and cartons of surgical cleaning clothes. "Last but not least is the recovery bay. Whatever nutrients the pups don't get from their mother, we provide in a proprietary blend formula. We breed the best, so they deserve the best to get them there."

The setup looked expensive and professionally organized. But some questions still nagged at Wyler. Why did Rafa set it up underground? Why the extra secrecy on his own property? Dog breeding wasn't illegal, unless...what they were doing with the dogs wasn't quite so legal. Wyler moved to the cages. A dog lunged at the metal gate. Froth flew from its mouth as it bared its teeth. An alarm tripped in Wyler's head as he continued walking past the cages. Each dog he passed displayed advanced signs of aggression. When he reached the last cage, his heart sank into his stomach. The dogs were all the same breed. Pit bulls. A breed of dog not inherently used for the type of personal protection Wyler was led to believe he was there to train. Wyler looked at

Soto, who stared at the floor and wouldn't meet his gaze. The twins stood by the next door. Wyler hoped beyond hope there weren't more dogs in the next room. If there were...

"Shall we continue?" Rafa said to Wyler.

Wyler swallowed, trying to maintain his composure. He didn't want to reveal his thoughts before he saw everything. "Lead the way," he said.

Rafa nodded at the twins, and they opened the next door.

"And this is our training facility," Rafa said, holding his arms out wide.

The area was double the width of the breeding room. In the center was a fenced-in square similar to what MMA fighters fought in. Circling it was a three-lane track but shrunk to fit the space. Directly to Wyler's left was a machine that looked like an industrial stove. Pipes jutted out of it and connected to eight oversized propane-looking tanks. Along the back wall was a row of treadmills.

"All of the dogs get exercised here," Rafa said. "If you have other requirements, don't hesitate to ask."

Rafa turned right and walked the perimeter of the facility. Wyler followed. Each step took him closer to realizing his fears about the bunker's purpose. The twins opened the next door along the same wall where they entered, but Wyler noticed another opposite. A rear exit, he guessed.

"Then we come to the main event," Rafa said, entering yet another new room. "We call this the Mexican Coliseum."

The floor dropped a good twelve feet lower than the others. The room contained six tiers of bench seating encircling a center ring constructed out of stones like an old well. Two men stood on opposing ends of the ring. One of them was a tall black guy, and the other was white and burly like a football lineman. They held chains that disappeared beyond the waist-high walls. Growls and an occasional barking fit bellowed out from the depths of the ring. Tenoch was the last one to enter the coliseum. The door closed behind him with a heavy clink of finality. Rafa walked down the steps toward the ring as he continued to talk.

"What do you think? Impressive, no?"

Wyler watched as the twins fanned out along the top tier of seats, looking down at Rafa like Roman sentries. The ring confirmed his fears. Wyler looked to Soto again, who still wouldn't meet his eye. The fog lifted, revealing the ugly sight of betrayal. Without many options, Wyler and Blackjack descended the steps with Soto and Tenoch in tow. As Wyler walked, his eyes scoured the room for exits. Aside from the door they entered, light glowed from an open corridor on the other side of the room. Giving up the high ground, though, would make an attempt at escape challenging, to say the least. For the moment, he needed to play things out.

"Yeah, it's impressive," Wyler said. "Business must be good."

"It is but there's room for growth," Rafa said, shaking his head. He patted the stones of the ring. "This here is where the future lies."

Wyler suppressed his rising rage. He knew what the ring was used for but wanted to hear Rafa say it. He wanted there to be no uncertainties before he tried to kill every last man in the vicinity. A red film momentarily blanketed his vision. His soul shook like a volcano, preparing to erupt and blast forth molten death. Wyler had unfortunately seen more atrocities committed against dogs in his life than he ever wanted. Using them for fighting was by far the worst. As horrible as the images were, he chose to never forget them. He used them as fuel and justification to do violent things to terrible men. Whether that was right or wrong wasn't for him to decide.

"Pit bulls aren't the ideal dog for personal protection," Wyler said.

Rafa and Tenoch exchanged a confused look.

"Personal protection?" Rafa said.

Wyler stared at Soto. His face had gone pale again. "That's what I was told I would be doing here."

"Is it, now?" Rafa said, shifting his focus to Soto as well. He sighed heavily. "No, Mr. Wyler, as I'm sure you've been able to piece together at this point, we need you to train our dogs to kill other dogs."

And there it was, in black and white. Soto had lied. Why? Wyler hoped he survived long enough to find out.

"I'm sorry, but I can't—" Wyler started but Soto interrupted.

"Training the dogs is to help protect your personal assets is what I told him," Soto said, stumbling forward, suddenly animated as if someone plunged a shot of adrenaline into his heart. "Trust me. He can do it. A dog is a dog. He trained them...I saw it first-hand... dogs taking down hardened Taliban fighters. This guy is the real deal. I mean, just look at the dog he brought." Soto stared at Wyler, his eyes pleading as he said, "I think you might have misunderstood part of what I told you. This isn't a problem, though, right?"

Wyler slowly shook his head, unable to keep the pity and disgust from his face. What had Soto done? A self-loathing washed over Wyler for ignoring his gut instincts. The money and his code of honor had blinded him into taking Soto at his word. And now he had to face the consequences head-on.

"What did he tell you?" Rafa said to Wyler.

Soto started, "That you needed—"

In a quick blur of motion, Rafa backhanded Soto across his face. The smack echoed off the stone walls. Soto staggered, caught off guard by the sudden blow. He rubbed his cheek in shock.

"I wasn't talking to you," Rafa said. "Mr. Wyler, it's important I know what exactly was communicated to you so that we are all operating toward the same end goal."

Wyler saw the desperation leaking from Soto's face. Whatever Soto was involved with, he was in deep. But he knew if Soto had told him the truth upfront, he would have said no. Hence the lie. Hence the guilt trip over an unpaid debt. He was banking on Wyler being unable to refuse once put on the spot. It was a clever trick he fell for, leaving him with two options.

One, he could fall in line with whatever apparent lie Soto had fed Rafa, but that didn't solve the bigger problem. There was zero chance Wyler would train any dog to kill another. It went against everything he believed in and stood for. Then his mind flicked to the stove he saw in the training room. Its use was apparent now. Any dogs that lost a fight or didn't meet their breeding standards must have been fed to the flames. The whole concept sickened Wyler.

His second option, the truth, didn't leave him with many good outs. Rafa, Tenoch, and the twins didn't seem like men who were opposed to violence. This was clear, since they were breeding dogs for fighting. If he declined to help, would they just let him walk away with a pat on the back? No hard feelings. Wyler doubted that very much.

"Yeah," Wyler said. "He told me about the pit bulls."

"Nothing else?"

"No."

"He didn't tell you why we need them trained with your set of skills? Or what's at stake for my business?"

"He just told me you were a real estate agent and now did land deals."

"I see," Rafa arched an eyebrow. "So, you would have no hesitation training our dogs to rip each other's throats out?"

Wyler shrugged. He didn't possess the natural gifts of acting like Soto did. He could bluff at cards, but this was different. More than money was at stake. If Rafa wasn't convinced by Wyler's answers, it could cost him everything.

"As long as I still get the money I was promised," Wyler said. "Then yeah, like Soto said, a dog's a dog."

Rafa stared at Wyler like he was trying to solve a quantum equation. His eyes narrowed.

"No," he said. "I'm not sure I believe you."

Soto, still rubbing his face, said, "Rafa, he—"

"Stop." Rafa raised his hand, halting any further debate.

"I'm sure Mr. Wyler is everything you described him to be," Rafa said. "And seeing his companion, I think he could help us with our problem and what we need." He walked a few steps closer to Wyler. "Would you do it for money, though? No. I don't think so. You have a moral objection to what we're doing here, don't you?"

Wyler didn't move or break his eye contact with Rafa. His expression remained neutral, but he didn't respond. Anything he said would only come across as disingenuous.

"But maybe I'm wrong," Rafa said, grinning. "So, let's find out."

Rafa turned, snapped his fingers, then pointed at the two men holding the chains leading into the ring. The men released the slack on the leashes, shouting as they did. Tenoch pushed Wyler in the back, forcing him forward. They wanted him to watch. Wyler willed his legs to move. At the edge of the ring, he reluctantly peered down. Two pit bulls—one black, one gray—thrashed violently, snarling in a blind rage. The dogs threw themselves at each other without any goal other than pure survival. They possessed plenty of aggression but lacked discipline. For Wyler, the sight was worse than watching a hundred horror movies. Out of the corner of his eye, he noticed Rafa wasn't looking at the dogs. His focus was on Wyler, studying him closely. It took all of Wyler's strength to avoid reacting when all he wanted to do was dive into the ring and stop the fighting.

The black pit bull landed a blow that drew blood from the gray pit bull's forehead. At that point, Rafa snapped his fingers again. The two men grabbed the chains and pulled, separating the dogs.

"Tell me now," Rafa said to Wyler. "This doesn't bother you?"

Wyler's jaw clenched as he shook his head.

"No? Hmm. How about this, then?"

Rafa nodded at Tenoch, who stepped past Wyler. As Tenoch approached the ring, he drew a gun from his hip. The Lineman restraining the gray pit bull yanked harder on the chain, lifting the dog off his front paws and bringing its head next to the top of the wall. Tenoch removed a silencer from a pocket and slowly began spinning it onto the barrel of the gun. His eyes never left Wyler's as he did so. Wyler's heart seized. He knew what was coming. The dog wheezed from the metal links cutting into its massive neck. Rafa was forcing Wyler's hand. The decision he needed to make tore him up inside. He had to either continue the lie or come clean and suffer the consequences.

Once the silencer was secured, Tenoch stepped to the side and raised the gun, leveling it at the dog's head. Sweat pooled at

Wyler's back. His stomach tightened. They were playing a game of chicken with him, and at the last second, Wyler was the one who swerved.

"Stop," Wyler said.

Rafa held up his hand, momentarily halting Tenoch from pulling the trigger.

"You said stop?"

Wyler glared at Tenoch. The dog's wheezing tore at Wyler's soul.

"Yes," Wyler said, seething, trying to control his rage.

"I thought so," Rafa said, frowning. He waved off Tenoch, who lowered the gun. The Lineman loosened his hold on the chain, and the pit bull dropped to all fours. It hacked uncontrollably as the air rushed back into its lungs.

Rafa sighed heavily, massaging his mangled ear as he looked at Soto. "Tomás, I gave you a chance...as a friend...and this...this is what my generosity gets me." He shook his head as he faced Wyler. "Mr. Wyler, this is an unfortunate position that Tomás has put us all in."

"He won't say anything," Soto said. "Neither of us will. You can trust him. We'll go. I'll find a way to make this right."

Rafa tilted his head slightly. "How can I trust him when I don't trust you? No. No. Neither of you are going anywhere. We've wasted too much time already. We're on a course that there's no deviating from." Rafa walked to Tenoch's side. "Mr. Wyler, you're going to help us. I'll give you until the morning to decide how willingly that's going to happen." He put his hand on Tenoch's shoulder. "Put them in the lounge."

Tenoch grinned as he casually aimed his gun at Wyler's chest.

"Rafa," Soto shouted. "Rafa, it doesn't have to be like this. Rafa!"

His pleas fell on deaf ears. Rafa climbed the steps toward the twins. He whispered something to them, then disappeared through the open corridor. Each twin produced a pistol from their waistband behind their backs. The Snake-tattooed guy kept his gaze trained on Wyler as he circled to the door they had entered the arena through, cutting off an escape avenue.

The situation was bleak. Wyler was outnumbered. Five against two, possibly three. He didn't know anymore where Soto's loyalties lay. Wyler assessed his odds of leaving the room alive if he made a move. The guns, number of guys, and the positional disadvantage swung the odds to a ninety percent chance of Wyler dying in a hail of bullets. Tenoch was about eight feet away. Wyler could give the command for Blackjack to go for him. The surprise could work. If it did, would Wyler be able to get the gun from him and take out the twins before they landed a lethal shot? Again, it didn't seem likely. No, he needed to bide his time and wait for a better chance to strike.

"Wyler..." Soto's voice sounded drained.

"Don't," Wyler said.

Tenoch flicked the barrel of his gun toward the open corridor. "Up the stairs," he said. Then he pointed the gun at Blackjack. "Try anything stupid, and I shoot the dog first. I've had a lot of practice at it, in case you were wondering."

"Good for you," Wyler said, heading for the stairs. Blackjack growled as he stared down Tenoch.

"You too, asshole," Tenoch said to Soto.

At the top of the stairs, the Scorpion-tattooed guy stood well out of reach of Wyler. He kept both hands on the gun, close to his chest with the barrel forward, ready to fire at a second's notice. It was the mark of someone well-trained from law enforcement or the military. Not good. When Wyler got to the entrance of the new corridor, Tenoch said, "Stop there."

The Snake made his way over and positioned himself in front of Wyler, gun aimed at center mass. Tenoch prodded Soto forward until he was two feet behind Wyler.

"Go," Tenoch said.

The Snake slowly backpedaled into the corridor. From Wyler's vantage point, the path went thirty feet before turning ninety degrees to the right. The quarters were tighter, so they had to walk single file, which presented an opportunity. It didn't leave him much time for planning. He had until they hit the turn to commit to the fluidly developing idea or wait for another chance to appear.

"Move," Tenoch said. He was at the rear of the line, behind the Scorpion, who was behind Soto. A gap of roughly four feet separated each of them. It could work, Wyler thought. They wanted him alive for the time being. That point factored into his decision. Time to shove all of his chips on the table.

Wyler caught Soto's eye, then made the slightest of head nods. Casually, he dropped his hands behind his back, quickly made the ok symbol with his right hand, and then brought them to his sides. He started to walk, hoping Soto picked up on the cue that he would make a move.

His pulse quickened. He counted each step to steady his nerves and slow his breathing. Things were going to happen fast. Timing and a little luck needed to be on his side to pull off the stunt without getting shot. As Wyler swung his right hand forward, his fingers brushed against Blackjack's ear. He did it two more times, all in rhythm with his gait to be unnoticeable to the Scorpion. The gesture signaled to Blackjack he was about to receive an attack command.

Wyler continued down the corridor, counting steps, as he slipped his right hand into his pocket. His fingers looped into the knuckleduster. Ten more steps to go. Sweat formed on Wyler's back, and his temples throbbed as his heart rate increased. No breathing exercises would slow it. Adrenaline began to seep into his bloodstream. He was going to need it. The Snake peered over his shoulder to gauge the distance of the upcoming turn. Five more steps...three more...Wyler slowed his pace to add whatever separation he could in the final seconds before the Snake disappeared around the corner. And as soon as he did, Wyler made his move.

Chapter 6

When the Snake-tattooed guy vanished around the corner, Wyler spun, crouched, and lunged at Soto with his left hand extended like a rugby player. At the same time, he shouted to Blackjack, "Go!"

Without hesitation, Blackjack sprang forward just as the Snake came back around the corner. Blackjack leaped, jaws spread wide. His teeth pierced flesh as they clamped down on the unsuspecting tattooed twin's wrist. The Snake yelled in pain as he staggered backward into the wall. His gun went off twice. The sudden burst of gunfire in tight quarters sent a sharp ringing through Wyler's eardrums as the bullets pinged off the stone bricks. The ringing continued as Wyler dug his feet in and pushed Soto into the Scorpion-tattooed guy.

As Wyler had hoped, the unexpected movement caught everyone off guard. The Scorpion didn't have enough time to process the situation and lock in on a target before Soto crashed into him. Tenoch shouted and backpedaled as the twin and Soto dropped. As they went down, Wyler stayed low. Then he dove over them like an Olympic swimmer, loaded his right arm, and fired it directly into Tenoch's chest. The impact of the titanium knuckleduster meeting bone reverberated through Wyler's wrist. Tenoch's mouth opened wide as all the air rushed from his lungs. Wyler's momentum slammed them to the ground.

Through the ringing in his ears, Wyler heard the Snake's shouts turning to screams. He could picture the damage Blackjack was inflicting on the man's arm. If it wasn't broken from the initial bite, the follow-up thrashing sure as hell wouldn't feel nice. Too bad for him. With a glance, Wyler looked toward his feet. Soto lay on his back like an overturned turtle on top of the Scorpion. His arms flailed blindly over his head, trying to grab hold of the Scorpion's gun. Wyler cocked his leg and fired a savage kick into the twin's skull, eliciting a groan. Before Wyler could process the damage he inflicted, pain exploded in his neck and shoulders. Tenoch had swung both his arms down in a chopping motion, striking the tender spot above Wyler's collarbone. The pain rippled up Wyler's neck into his brain. Tenoch's right knee then shot into Wyler's ribs. He was lucky, though. Their close proximity didn't allow for much force to be generated.

Wyler rolled with the blow and threw a haymaker that connected with the side of Tenoch's face. The knuckleduster opened a gash. Blood gushed from the fresh wound. Seizing the moment, Wyler scrambled forward and lodged his left forearm into Tenoch's throat. Tenoch wheezed from the pressure as his right hand searched for his gun while his left clawed at Wyler's face. Wyler swung his fist again. The titanium freight trained into

Tenoch's temple. The body immediately went slack as Tenoch's eyes rolled into unconsciousness.

Panting, Wyler pressed himself to a standing position. He whipped around and quickly surveyed the situation. Soto was on his knees, now straddling the Scorpion. His hands were crossed in an X, each gripping the fabric of the twin's shirt. It was a military technique used to choke someone out. It was clear the twin was already down for the count. Wyler tapped Soto rapid-fire on the shoulder.

"He's down, he's down," Wyler said, pulling him off the guy. "Leave him. We need to go now."

Soto's head jolted up. His eyes were wild and unfocused. Tears streaked down his cheeks as he bared his teeth. It was the look of a man prepared to kill anything in his path to ensure his own survival. Wyler knew the look from his time in the shit overseas.

"Leave him," Wyler repeated, yanking Soto to his feet. "Come on. Move."

They climbed over the limp bodies. Blackjack skirted to the left and right, dodging the unwieldy fists of the Snake. The wrist remained locked in his jaws. Wyler scooped the pistol off the ground, flipped it so he clutched the barrel, and then hammered the butt of the gun into the twin's forehead. His head snapped back, and then he sagged to a seated position. His limbs twitched as unconsciousness took hold of him.

"Release," Wyler shouted, and Blackjack obeyed. "Good boy."

Wyler's heart was pumping. He felt a stress headache forming at the base of his skull.

"Do you know how to get out of here?" Wyler said to Soto. "Do you know where this hallway leads?"

Soto's face was pale. He bent over and wretched. As he wiped his mouth with the back of his hand, he nodded. "This way," he said and stumbled forward.

"On me," Wyler said to Blackjack. "Search."

Blackjack squeezed past them and sprinted down the corridor. Wyler clutched the back of Soto's shirt and hurried him forward. Forty feet ahead, Blackjack stopped at a door along the left wall.

"There?" Wyler said.

Soto looked up. "No. That's a lounge. Keep going straight. This loops around to where we came in."

Blackjack stood at attention, eager for his next order. Wyler waved two fingers together, directing him to keep going. Blackjack did as instructed. Wyler glanced over his shoulder, expecting to see Tenoch and the twins back on their feet with guns raised. In the narrow corridor, they'd be easy to pick off. He tamped down the fears and kept going. Ahead, the path made another ninety-degree right turn. As he was trained, Blackjack barreled ahead. The sight caused Wyler to hold his breath. Over his storied military career, he'd seen dogs disappear around corners in hostile environments hundreds of times. After losing two dogs in the line of duty, a part of his mind that he tried unsuccessfully to suppress feared the worst.

Ten seconds later, Wyler hauled Soto to a stop at the corner. Controlling his breath, Wyler peered around the edge of the wall. Seeing no one, he rushed out. The corridor went straight. An open section cut left halfway down.

"The turn ahead," Soto said, pointing. "That's our way out."

"Alright," Wyler said. "Blackjack, on me."

Each second he didn't see the dog, his heart skipped a beat. Wyler told himself there would have been screaming if Black-jack had found someone. He got to the halfway point and saw the exit door.

"On me," Wyler repeated.

Five seconds later, Blackjack appeared at the end of the corridor. He trotted to Wyler's side.

"Good boy," Wyler said, patting Blackjack on the side. "Good boy." A sense of relief overcame him. "Let's get out of here."

At the door, Wyler pushed on it, but it didn't budge.

"The button there," Soto said, pointing at a red button to the right of the door that looked like it would launch a nuclear warhead. "Hit it."

Wyler smacked his palm on it. Internal bolts retracted, and the door popped ajar. As he was pushing it open, Wyler suddenly felt something sharp stab him between his shoulder blades. It almost felt like a bee sting. Then, the wall began to bend, and his vision blurred. He reached for the spot where he felt the sting but found it difficult to coordinate his movements. Eventually, his fingers curled around a smooth object. He yanked whatever it was out, then stared at a projectile dart. A fog enveloping his mind made it difficult for him to process what the object was. He turned and noticed Soto on the ground, lying on his side. A figure stood at the end of the corridor. Through his hazy vision, Wyler could just make out Rafa lowering a stainless steel gun. And then Wyler's mind clicked the pieces together. A tranquilizer. Panic seized his chest, realizing what was happening. He attempted a step, but his legs weighed a million pounds.

"Blackjack," Wyler managed to get out. "Hide."

He wanted to say more, but the chemicals spreading through his veins dragged him into total darkness.

The haze slowly lifted. Wyler had no idea how much time had

passed since being hit with the dart. He shook his head and blinked a few times before his vision came back into focus. Table-top lamps cast a soft golden light over the windowless room. Directly in front of him was a grand bar that looked like it had been stolen from an Ivy League college watering hole. Eight ornate stools stood regally before it, awaiting customers. Craft liquor bottles rested on shelves behind the bar. A Mexican flag draped along the wall to the left, and an American flag was to the right. Roughly fifteen feet separated Wyler from the bar.

He sat in a plush black leather chair in the corner of the room. His wrists were bound with a thin gray wire that dug into his skin. Carefully, he wriggled his forearms, testing the hold of the binding. There was no give. He felt pressure around his ankles, indicating they were bound as well. His mouth was dry, and his shoulders throbbed. A groan came from his right. Soto sat wrapped in a similar chair five feet away. His head rolled from side to side as he came to. Then his body went rigid, and his eyes burst open. He jerked frantically against his restraints.

"Relax," Wyler said.

Soto stopped and scanned the room until he spotted Wyler. Then, his body sagged.

"Fuck, man, I thought I was dead," Soto said.

"Not yet, anyway."

"What happened?"

"Tranquilizer dart is my guess. Probably keep them on hand for the dogs."

"Shit." Soto looked around a little more. "Where's... where's Blackjack?"

"I don't know. For your sake, though, you better hope nothing happens to him."

Soto stared at his knees. He mumbled, "I'm sorry, brother."

"What the fuck is this, Soto? What are you involved in?"

Soto shook his head and shrugged. His lips moved like he was going to talk, then stopped. After a heavy sigh, he said, "You remember when we were in the South during our last campaign?"

Wyler frowned. He wanted answers, not more reminiscing. "I don't care about that. Why are we here?"

"It's part of it," Soto said, still staring at his knees. "Do you remember that time in the South or what?"

Wyler inhaled and decided to let Soto talk. "Yeah. I remember."

"I took that fall, tweaked my back?"

"Yeah."

"Well, it never really healed right. I dealt with it for a while once I got out. About three years ago, the pain got so bad that I had to get surgery. Turns out I messed up some discs or some shit. Anyway, after the surgery...I got hooked on the pain meds. Fucking oxy, brother. Those things are no joke. I didn't think it was a problem at first...I thought I could handle it, but I couldn't. That feeling...I hadn't felt that good in years. And I started chasing it, chasing that feeling. And I couldn't stop." He paused and shifted slightly in the chair. He grit his teeth at the pressure from the bindings.

"Why didn't you tell me?" Wyler said. "You could've reached out."

"And said what? 'I'm hooked on pills, come help me.' Come on, man." Soto shook his head again. "I was a Marine. I was supposed to be able to handle my own shit. You know how it is with guys like us. All that macho bullshit. We don't get help. We stuff it down deep and deal with it. Sack up."

A sadness pushed against some of Wyler's rage for Soto getting him into the situation they found themselves in. He understood where Soto was coming from. The same mindset had been drilled into him. Mental health for vets, unfortunately, wasn't the military's forte. He'd lost others who had gone down the same road Soto described.

"So, what happened?"

"I started missing appointments and showings. Then, I started losing listings. And as my need for the pills grew, my bank account dwindled." He shrugged, then looked up. His gaze was far away. "I got into an ugly cycle. I resorted to gambling more to try and scrounge up more money for more pills. And that just became another addiction. Once, I was out here in Vegas on a bender and met up with Rafa. We were catching up on old times...one thing led to another...and he brought me here."

Soto blinked, then faced Wyler. His eyes were wide with self-loathing. "And I bet on the dog fights. Like a piece of shit, I bet. I even cheered. I didn't care about the animals. I just saw it as another way to try and win money and get my pills."

Wyler nodded, taking in the story. Pieces of it still didn't fit, though.

"Okay," Wyler said. "But why me?"

"Competition..." Soto grunted and tilted his head back slightly. "What group built this city?"

"What?"

"Who built Las Vegas? Originally."

"You talking about the mafia?"

"Exactly. Their stranglehold was mostly busted up, though, in the eighties. Corporations took over a lot of the casinos. But there was this guy, John Agosti...he was the son of a family with a less visible role out here that flew under the radar. Agosti goes to Stanford, gets into real estate, and builds up a big name for himself. On the surface, everything he does is above board. But below the surface, he's still tied to organized crime."

"How do you know all this?" Wyler asked.

"You build a big network of friends and associates as a real estate agent. I got close with a guy who's up there in the ranks under Agosti. Dan Hunter. Turns out he's a gambler too. We bet some dogs together...Agosti has a dog operation..." Soto closed his eyes, and his head drooped.

"Hey," Wyler said. "You good?"

"Yeah...sorry...my head feels like someone jammed a bag of cotton balls in there."

"Keep going."

"Rafa and Agosti...they both want to buy a huge chunk of land. It's in an area with access to water, which, out here, means a hell of a lot. With the amount they could develop there...for them, the land is worth billions."

Wyler rotated his wrists. The wires bit in. He didn't know how long they had before Tenoch or the twins would return. And if he were going to die, Wyler wanted to at least know why.

"Move it along," Wyler said.

"They've been fighting, Rafa and Agosti. It started through legal means, but as the situation stalemated, they dipped into not-so-legal methods to win. One of Rafa's buildings got burnt to the ground, so then one of Agosti's chief architects disappeared. Each incident led to a new incident, and..."

"They went to war," Wyler said. "Is Rafa connected then, too?"

"I've only heard rumors. His father was supposedly a big shot with the cartels in Mexico during the late nineties. Whether Rafa is backed by them today...I don't know...but if Agosti hasn't offed him, there has to be a reason."

"He doesn't want the full weight of the cartels coming after him."

Soto shrugged. "Could be. Both sides have to walk a careful line. And this isn't like the old days. Vegas is supposed to be reputable and safe. When bodies start turning up, it's not good for anyone."

"The cops don't step in?"

"From Hunter and the innuendos I've heard, both sides have a few cops on their payrolls. But it's got to the point where even they can't contain the questions being asked. That brings unwanted attention. That brings the government. Not good. So Rafa and Agosti made a bet."

Wyler was beginning to see how the trail led to him. "The dogs?"

"The dogs," Soto nodded. "Both of them breed pit bulls for brawling. So they put the land deal against a couple of dogs fighting. If you can believe that shit. Whoever's dogs lost would agree to withdraw from the bids for the land rights. And on top of that, they'd have to pay fifty million dollars in restitution for damages done during their warring days."

Wyler sighed. "And you volunteered my name to train them."

Soto went back to staring at his knees. "Yeah. I remembered everything you did with those dogs overseas. You were a legend, brother."

"What was in it for you?"

"What I told you in AC. I'd be the agent for any properties Rafa developed there. I needed the money. I saw an opportunity and went for it. If I got you on board to train the dogs and they won the fights, then Rafa would give me what I wanted. I could dig my way out."

Something still didn't fit for Wyler. "That still doesn't fully explain why me? They didn't have anyone else to train the dogs?"

"They're relatively new to the scene here. That psycho fuck, Tenoch, he deals more with the breeding end of the operation. His training methods, though, leave a lot to be desired. And Agosti knew that, which is why he pushed for that specific bet. So, I offered you up to Rafa, and he went for it."

"Uh-huh."

"It's like any sport. When your team is playing like shit, you bring in a new coach to try to win a championship. Think of it like the Jets bringing in Bill Belichick to turn their fortunes around."

"That's how you sold it?"

Soto nodded.

"But you knew I would be against dog fighting," Wyler said. "That's why you lied and told me it was to train protection dogs."

"I thought...I don't know...Maybe when you saw the whole setup out here...and the money...that you'd do it."

"Was the money offer even real?"

"Yeah."

"But looking for listings in AC, that was all bullshit?"

Soto nodded again.

"Then you told Rafa I had no issues with dog fighting," Wyler said. "And here we are. Why didn't you just ask me for money? I would've paid you back what I owed."

"It wouldn't have been enough. I fucked up, brother. My head wasn't right. You got every right to hate me. I broke your trust... our friendship...I—"

"Stop," Wyler said.

He'd heard enough. What was done was done. No apology was going to change that fact. Wyler sat there quietly, lost in a whirlwind of thoughts. Blackjack's safety was at the top of his mind. Like all his dogs, he and Blackjack had formed a bond tighter than a father and son. Wyler closed his eyes and tried to create a mental map of the area. Mostly desert, which at least blended with the color of Blackjack's fur. It would make him harder to spot. Plus, he had given him the 'hide' command. It was a game they played since Blackjack was a puppy. As Blackjack aged, they refined the process. On some outings, it took Wyler over an hour to find him. He wondered if Rafa or Tenoch would have sent people out to search for him. They want you, not the dog, he tried to reassure himself. If Tenoch caught him...what they would do to him...Wyler forced the thought away. It wasn't productive.

"They're going to kill us, aren't they?" Soto said. The comment broke the silence like an exploding landmine. It snapped Wyler out of his meandering thoughts. "Even if you help and give them what they want...they won't risk letting you go to tell someone about it. And me... I'm already dead."

Wyler had considered the same line of thinking. Hearing the words out loud made it real. While Wyler agreed with the sentiment, he needed to stay positive. If he was still breathing, there was a chance of escape, no matter how slim the odds. And as much as Soto had screwed him over, Wyler still saw him as a resource.

"Yeah, they might try," Wyler said. "But so have a lot of bigger and badder people in the past. And who's still standing?"

Soto grunted and shook his head.

"Say it," Wyler said. "I need to hear you say it."

Soto hesitated, then said, "We are."

"That's right. Now, what else do you know about this place?"

Wyler wanted to keep Soto thinking and talking. If he fully receded into himself, then he'd be useless.

"I don't know," Soto said. "We walked through the whole place."

"What about exits?"

He thought for a second, then said, "There's one at the back of the training facility. Stairs lead up through a hatchway."

"Alright, that's something. Any other—"

Before Wyler finished the question, the door swung open. The Scorpion-tattooed twin walked in first, followed by the Snake twin, whose left arm was wrapped in a thick cast. Tenoch entered last and closed the door. A patch covered his cheek where the knuckleduster had opened it up. His face was worn, and a lump rose at his temple. A small surge of defiant pride swelled in Wyler's chest at the ragged state of his captors. If this was to be the final minutes of his life, he was happy that he went out swinging.

Chapter 7

The twins edged into the room. They carried with them a medical stench of rubbing alcohol and peroxide, most likely from treating their wounds. A dark satisfaction lined their faces like jurors handing down a death penalty verdict to a serial rapist. Murder twinkled in their eyes, brighter than a phosphorus spark. Their cold, predatory stares triggered in Wyler a terrifying premonition of what was to come. Despite the claustrophobic sensation of oncoming trauma tightening around him, Wyler greeted them with a grin. Show them no fear, no weakness. Get under their skin and force them into making a mistake he could benefit from. They want you alive—for now—Wyler reminded himself, hardening his defenses for whatever they threw at him.

Tenoch brushed past the twins and sat on the lip of the coffee table in front of Wyler and Soto. He studied them one at a time for five seconds. Trying to intimidate them, Wyler guessed. That wasn't going to work.

"I'll take a whiskey. Neat," Wyler said. "I see a bottle of Blanton's back there. That'll do nicely."

Tenoch turned toward the bar, then refocused on Wyler with a smile. The motion seemed to agitate his facial wounds. Good, Wyler thought. He hoped it hurt like hell.

"That's cute," Tenoch said.

"What about appetizers? Salted peanuts, maybe?"

Tenoch remained expressionless while his hand slowly disappeared into his jacket pocket. Then, in a quick burst, his right hand shot out, and he lunged. Wyler heard the clicking a split second before he felt the pain. An explosion of electricity rippled through his body. The shock was so sudden it took his breath away. All of his muscles seized as he jerked violently in the chair. The wire bindings sank into his flesh. After what felt like an eternity, Tenoch returned to a seated position on the coffee table. Hatred stoked the flames in his eyes once again. Wyler's mouth tasted like dirty pennies. A high-pitched ringing echoed through his ears. His heart thundered against his chest, screaming to be slowed.

As the air returned to Wyler's lungs and his muscles uncoiled, he spotted the black taser in Tenoch's hand. The two metal prongs protruding from the device's top gleamed like snake fangs, eager to inflict more torment. Tenoch cupped his left hand to his ear and leaned toward Wyler.

"Any more cute comments?" he said.

Wyler wished he could hurl one out, but the buzzsaw slicing through his brain prevented it.

"I didn't think so," Tenoch said.

He set the taser down on the coffee table, then rested both palms on the edge.

"So, here's where we stand after your little stunt earlier. Me. The boys back there," Tenoch jerked his thumb at the twins. He turned then and nodded at the Scorpion-tattooed twin. "That's Javier, by the way." Then he motioned to the Snake-tattooed one. "And that's Xolo." Tenoch faced Wyler again after the introductions. "Anyway, we'd like to tear you to pieces and feed you to the dogs. And who knows, maybe we still will. Rafa, though, he sees something in you. He's a good judge of people even after meeting them briefly. He also seems to buy the stories this sack of shit told him." Tenoch slapped a hand down on Soto's knee. Soto flinched, which drew a chuckle from Tenoch. "Frankly, I disagree with the decision. I think I was more than capable of beating a dog into a top contender."

"If you train as well as you fight," Wyler said. "I wouldn't bet on it."

The flames in Tenoch's eyes hit such a high temperature that their color shifted from orange to blue. His hand shot out again. The taser jabbed into Wyler's gut. Volts radiated through his sinews and up his spine. Wyler's teeth ground together with enough force he thought one might jar loose. As his body flailed, the wire cut deeper. Tenoch released the button and sat back. Wyler panted, desperate to catch his breath. He turned his head and spat on the floor. Sweat soaked his shirt.

"I can do this all day," Tenoch said. "Talk as much shit as you like."

Wyler's vision blurred, and the room spun. Darkness patiently waited by his side, ready to embrace him like a warm blanket. Bile rose up in his throat, but he forced it back down. His head rolled forward. All he could hear was blood passing through his skull at a molecular level, rushing past faster than a Formula 1 car. Then rough, dense knuckles slapped hard across Wyler's face. The jolt retracted the black curtain. He squinted his eyes, refocusing them on Tenoch. It was like escaping a nightmare and realizing you weren't dreaming. The nightmare was reality.

"Don't go passing out on me yet," Tenoch said.

Wyler inhaled deeply, then exhaled. He didn't know how much more of this he could endure.

"As I was saying," Tenoch continued. "Rafa wants to give you a shot despite my protests. As a consolation prize, though, I get the honor of using whatever means I see fit to persuade you to do the job and to do it well." Tenoch tapped the side of the taser on Wyler's thigh. "In a few minutes, I will ask you, 'Are you ready to get to work?'. Okay?"

Any sane person would jump at the chance to avoid more pain. Located in the recesses of Wyler's mind, the voice of reason pleaded with him: *Just train the dogs. Put aside your feelings and morality. Do the damn job that you know you can do. This is about surviving.* But then the voice of honor shouted from deep within Wyler's heart: *Do this, and there's no coming back. You'll never be able to look at yourself in the mirror again. Never compromise.*

"Now, before you answer," Tenoch said. "There's a stipulation you should hear first. I'm going to ask you only three times. That's it. No more, no less. After the third time, then I have no use for you, and I'll put you in the ground. Get it?"

Wyler stared at Tenoch but didn't say anything. Three chances. It wasn't much, but it was better than nothing. That meant he'd have three opportunities to come up with a plan.

"I said, do you get it?" Tenoch shouted and quickly jabbed the taser into Wyler's chest. The zap lasted less than three seconds, but it hurt as much as if it'd been on him for three minutes. A light smell of burning fabric drifted through the air.

"Yeah," Wyler mumbled through the pain. "Got it."

"Good dog," Tenoch said, grinning. He stood and patted Wyler on the head. As Tenoch removed his jacket, he nodded at the twins. "Now comes the part where we're going to do some persuading."

Wyler didn't like the sound of that. He knew whatever was coming wasn't going to be pleasant. For him, taking a beating required more mental stamina than physical. If he could transport himself into the safe places within his memories, then he could endure a surprising amount of violence. And when the pain got really bad, the challenge was to shut off the mind completely. The only solace Wyler took was that they still needed him functional if they wanted him to train the dogs. They could inflict damage, but not to the point where he was incapacitated. The same, though, couldn't be said for Soto.

Tenoch reached into his pocket and pulled out Wyler's knuckledusters. He studied the weapons like he had when he first discovered them on Wyler. He bounced them in his palm like he was weighing a sack of coins before sliding his fingers into the smoothly polished holes. Tenoch flicked his head at Javier, who walked behind Soto's chair. Javier grabbed Soto by the hair and forced his head up. Tenoch's eyes smoldered as he stared at Wyler.

"I'm going to show you how I train my dogs," Tenoch said. "Maybe we can compare notes."

"That's funny," Wyler said. "I didn't take you as someone who knew how to read or write."

Tenoch grinned as he shook his head. Then he planted his feet and hurled his fist into Soto's stomach. Soto's body released a sound like a water balloon bursting against asphalt. A right fist hooked and smashed into the side of Soto's face. Then, the left hand swung in, crashing into the other side of his face. Wyler watched helplessly as the beating ensued. He didn't look away, not wanting to give Tenoch any satisfaction that his techniques were effective. Tenoch worked over Soto's body with four more strikes and then a final one that connected with his nose. The sound of bone shattering struck Wyler in the heart. Soto had messed up, but he didn't deserve what he was getting. Guilt stepped into the fray of emotions battling inside Wyler. He had the power to stop the pummeling. All he needed to say was, *'I'll do it,'* and their suffering would cease. But only briefly. Death still loomed over them either way. So, then the question became, did he want to die with dignity or not?

Tenoch stepped back. His chest heaved from the exertion. He clinked the bloody knuckledusters together as he looked at Wyler.

"I like these," Tenoch said. "I can see the appeal now."

"Glad it makes you feel like a big man," Wyler said. He visualized breaking free of his restraints and snapping Tenoch's neck.

Javier released Soto's head. It sagged limply until his chin touched his chest. The twin wiped his hand on Soto's shirt, disgust plastered on his face. Tenoch crouched and gazed at Soto. He frowned, realizing he had passed out.

"See, I like to tenderize my dogs first," Tenoch said, spreading his fingers to remove the knuckledusters. "It lets them know who's in charge." He turned to Xolo. "Grab me a towel."

Xolo went to the bar and removed a towel from a hook. He handed it to Tenoch. Settling back onto the coffee table, Tenoch took his time wiping the blood from the knuckledusters. When he finished, he inspected them like a jeweler would a diamond.

"Good as new."

Gently, Tenoch placed them on the table and picked up his taser again.

"Alright then, consider this my first time asking," Tenoch said, locking eyes with Wyler. "Are you ready to get to work?"

Wyler didn't look away. He tensed his muscles, preparing for what he knew was going to come, then spat through gritted teeth, "Fuck. You."

Tenoch shrugged, his face dispassionately blank. "Okay. I'll take that as your first no." He got up once again, but this time slowly walked behind Wyler. The anticipation caused Wyler to break into a cold sweat. His whole body tensed, waiting. Each second was its own private nightmare. And then Tenoch struck. The prongs pricked his neck, and his senses were jolted into paralysis. He felt like he was being cooked alive. With his body overloaded, Wyler plummeted blissfully into darkness.

In the abyss of unconsciousness, Wyler floated back twenty-two years to when he was twelve in Atlantic City. It was a memory that was never far away. He was walking home from school, alone as usual, when he passed an alley. The distressed yipping of a dog, he remembered, was what caught his attention. It was one of those alleyways that butted up against another building, creating only one way in and one way out. The dog's cries unexplainably pulled him into the alley like some unseen being controlled him. He approached a dumpster. Behind it were four boys, at least two or three years older than him. They were huddled in the corner, shouting at something. Two of them carried baseball bats. As Wyler moved in closer, he saw what they were yelling at.

The boys had duct-taped a cat's hind legs together. It hissed as it hobbled around, struggling to find an avenue of escape. In front of the cat was a dog. It was black with streaks of tan fur. Based on the colors and the block-shaped head, Wyler guessed it was a Rottweiler. The dog wasn't very big, maybe just past the puppy phase at nine or ten months old. A leash made from rope was looped around the dog's neck. One of the boys, wearing a backward Jets hat, shouted at the dog. "Come on, kill it. Get it."

The dog whimpered as the boys jabbed their bats and kicked it in its haunches. The scene had a visceral effect on Wyler. Disgust blended with anger. Something he'd never felt before. His young mind could barely process the cruelty unfolding before his eyes. The cries of the animals tugged at a primal emotion deep inside him. When he stared into the dog's eyes, Wyler saw parts of himself. Neglected. Left to fend for himself against an unforgiving world. Most kids would have turned tail and booked it out of that alley. He guessed that some might have gone to get an adult, but not many. Wyler was outnumbered and outsized. The fight or flight mechanism ingrained in the DNA of humankind short-circuited in Wyler at that moment, forever changing him at his core. Flight was no longer an option. There was only fight.

Without realizing he was doing it, Wyler removed his backpack and swung it as hard as he could into the hamstrings of the biggest kid. The big kid dropped to his knees with a startled yelp. The other boys turned. Wyler capitalized on their surprise and sent his right leg into the second-biggest kid's groin. The kid dropped his bat as he crumpled to the pavement with a groan. The other two boys recovered from their initial shock and reacted. The one wearing the Jets hat dove at Wyler. He smelled like fried foods and sweat. They grappled awkwardly as kids with no fighting experience tended to do. Then Wyler felt hands grab him by the shoulders. The biggest kid yanked Wyler free and tossed him into the side of the Dumpster. The impact knocked the wind from his lungs. As he regained his balance, batter number two swung at Wyler's head. Wyler dodged, but not fast enough. The bat connected with part of his forehead, dropping him to all fours. His vision split into shards like a broken mirror, and the world spun beneath him. The thoughts swirling through his head skipped like a scratched CD. Then the biggest kid kicked Wyler in the ribs. Fire cascaded through his young body. Even then, the notion of flight was nowhere to be found.

Splayed out on his stomach, light gleamed off an object beneath the dumpster. He reached for it. His fingers curled around the neck of a beer bottle just as the biggest kid grabbed Wyler by the ankles.

"Who the fuck is this punk?" the biggest kid said, dragging Wyler into the open.

When the beer bottle cleared, Wyler smashed the end of it against the edge of the Dumpster. He spun and lashed out with the makeshift weapon like a writhing snake. The biggest kid cried out and immediately dropped Wyler's legs. Blood trickled down the biggest kid's forearms where the bottle struck. Fear flooded the kid's face. The other kids looked on in panic. Wyler scrambled shakily to his feet. He parried the beer bottle like a fencer's sword.

"This kid's fucking nuts," the biggest kid said.

Wyler growled, then staggered into a lunge. The kids darted away from him and sprinted down the alley. He swayed, waiting and watching to ensure they didn't return. Satisfied they were gone, Wyler clumsily rooted out a stack of newspapers from the Dumpster. He used them to pin down the cat while he sliced through the duct tape with the beer bottle. When the tape separated, the cat hissed and then scurried off in a blur. As the adrenaline waned, Wyler's legs felt about as solid as sand. He sat on the ground with his back against the brick wall. He closed his eyes, but that made the spinning worse.

A dragging sound to his left caught his attention.

The dog crept forward with its tail between its legs. Wyler held out his hand and said, "It's alright. I won't hurt you."

The dog hesitated, then shuffled forward with the rope in tow. It stopped a few inches from Wyler's hands. Carefully, he sniffed Wyler's fingers before taking another step closer.

"It's alright," Wyler repeated. Then, he slowly reached out and petted the dog's head. "See, not so bad. Let's get this off of you." The dog allowed Wyler to unloop the rope and slip it off. Once freed, the dog leaped onto Wyler's chest and licked his face. The pain and dizziness evaporated instantaneously under the onslaught. Love was all it wanted. Even at that young age, Wyler remembered the sensation crystalizing something profound inside his heart. A bond that could never be broken. Wyler held the dog closely as he rubbed its back, then whispered, "Don't worry, you're safe now."

Wyler left the memory behind as his eyes blinked open. His stomach tightened when he spotted Tenoch sitting at the bar, sipping from a rocks glass. Wyler glanced at Soto. The blood from his busted nose had dried in a gruesome trail down his mouth and chin. Black and blue rings were beginning to show beneath his eyes. The amount of time Wyler was out eluded him, but based on the dried blood on Soto's face, he guessed it was no more than a half hour. Tenoch watched Wyler while he finished his drink. Javier leaned against the wall, swiping through his phone. Next to him were two long poles with wire loops at the end. A leather couch rested against the wall opposite the door. Xolo sat there, picking a loose gauze thread wrapped around his damaged arm. A duffle bag occupied the seat next to him. Laying across the top was an Uzi machine gun with a silencer affixed to the barrel. Clearly, they had a new approach in store to persuade Wyler to take the job.

"You awake now, big dog?" Tenoch said, setting his glass down.

Wyler didn't fire back a remark. He wanted to see what was going to happen next. If an escape route presented itself, he didn't want to be any stiffer from another taser strike. Tenoch stood and walked over.

"We're going to have a little change of scenery," Tenoch said. He waved his hand like a general sending a legion into battle. Javier pushed off the wall. He handed one of the poles to Tenoch. Xolo got up from the couch, secured the Uzi in his non-damaged hand, and moved to the side where he had a clear line of fire. Javier walked behind Soto, looped the wire over his head, then tightened it around his throat. It was a tool used to catch dogs. Tenoch, standing behind Wyler, did the same thing. The wire cinched tight, making it challenging to swallow, let alone breathe.

"Xolo here is going to cut you two loose," Tenoch said. "Any bullshit like before, and we'll put you down. Understand?"

Wyler nodded, and Soto grunted.

"Good dogs," Tenoch said.

Xolo dipped his head into the sling attached to the gun, then let it dangle by his side. From his back pocket, he removed a pair of wire cutters. Tenoch pulled Wyler's neck restraint taught as Xolo crouched with the cutters. Two snips and Wyler's ankles were free. Two more and then his hands. A small sigh of relief left Wyler's lips from the release of pressure against his wrists. Wyler weighed the odds of making a move. He could thrust backward, but the pole would be too unwieldy to deal with, even if he managed to knock it loose from Tenoch's grip. And Xolo kept glancing at Wyler. The first escape attempt put them on high alert for another try. Bottom line then, the odds were stacked too high against him. Once Soto was freed from the chair, Xolo quickly stepped back and brought the gun to the ready.

"Alright, dogs," Tenoch said. "On your feet."

Tenoch manipulated the pole with skill, guiding Wyler out of the chair. Wyler's legs felt like hardening jelly. Going vertical sent a rush of blood through his system, causing him to sway. But Tenoch compensated for the dip and kept Wyler upright. After slinging the duffle bag over his shoulder, Xolo opened the door and backpedaled. He glared at Wyler, almost begging him to try something so he'd have an excuse to riddle his body with bullets.

"We're going right," Tenoch said.

They returned to the arena. The wire nearly strangled Wyler as he tapped his toes on the steps so as not to fall down them. When they got to the other side, Xolo opened the door to the training facility. He continued straight and approached the exit door Soto had mentioned. Lights flickered on, illuminating a staircase going up. Xolo climbed to the top, where he shouldered open a hatchway. A flood of sunlight burst in. Wyler squinted against the intensity as Tenoch prodded him forward. Hot air blasted Wyler in the face as he emerged into the desert. The warmth felt good after being underground for how long? Wyler tried to locate the sun. He spotted it to his left, hanging about an hour before noon. That meant he'd been in the bunker for roughly fourteen hours since arriving at Rafa's house. Getting out of the cramped confines and into the expanse of the desert breathed new life into Wyler. But his hope was short lived. After walking fifty yards, Tenoch forced Wyler to his knees. He stared into a dugout hole, a grave big enough for two bodies.

Chapter 8

Javier forced Soto to the ground next to Wyler. From the corner of his eye, Wyler saw Soto's focus go to the grave. He exhaled audibly at the sight. Wyler knew what Soto was thinking. Death was upon them.

"My father used to work for Rafa's father in Tijuana," Tenoch began.

He released the pole, and it clanked to the dirt at Wyler's feet. The weight made Wyler tilt his head back to relieve the tension around his neck. Tenoch walked in a wide arch, stopping at the pile of dirt dug from the grave. The smell of drying decay wafted through the air.

"After my father was killed by the Federales..." Tenoch said, making the sign of the cross. "... Rafa's father took me in. Armando. Everyone just called him Mando. I was only seven. Javier. Xolo. They share similar stories as mine." Tenoch studied the pile of dirt while he removed his button-down shirt. When it was off, he spread it over the heap and then sat down. "Mando was a great leader. He taught me many life lessons. His greatest strength, though, was the ability to find the pain point that lies in us all. And once he found it, he owned you. In his line of work, it was a crucial skill to possess."

Wyler couldn't care less about Tenoch's story. He knew it was part of the scare tactic. The more he rambled on, the more the victim thought about how they could avoid ending up in the grave. Guys in Wyler's platoon had done the same thing overseas. Wyler didn't necessarily condone its use, but it was hard to argue with the results.

"One day Mando picked me up—I was, I don't know, sixteen—and he brought me to this place where they fought dogs," Tenoch said. "They called it The Well because a stone ring was dug into the ground like a ... like a well." Tenoch smiled at the repetition as he stared into the distance. "Inside the well were two dogs. Some of the meanest fucked up dogs I've ever seen. They were chained to be just out of reach of one another. Mando didn't feed them for four days. The dogs were out of their minds by the time we showed up."

While Tenoch talked, Wyler assessed his surroundings for any hint of a chance to break free. Javier and Xolo had moved behind him and Soto. The pole prevented Wyler from turning his head far enough to see their exact locations. He assumed both Javier and Tenoch also had guns on them. Wyler's hands weren't bound, which was a plus, and the pole could serve as a weapon. The only problem was they were in too much open space. Even if he managed to get five yards away without getting shot, there was no place to hide. The mountains were still at least six miles off. His second assessment found the risks still too high. He remained alert, though, for any changes.

"I'm not boring you, am I?" Tenoch said to Wyler.

"No, keep going," Wyler said. "I was just about to fall asleep."

"You've got cojones. I'll give you that," Tenoch laughed. "Don't worry, I'm almost at the best part of the story." Tenoch scooped a handful of dirt as he continued to talk. "Mando had two people already there. A local official and one of his two sons. You see, the official didn't want to approve a bill that would have benefited one of Mando's legitimate businesses. The guy wouldn't take a bribe like all the rest did." Tenoch looked at Wyler and nodded. "Sort of like you. He grew a conscience and decided the cartels weren't good for the community. That he was somehow above it." Tenoch shook his hand back and forth like a gold miner's pan, letting the dirt tumble back to the earth. "So we're there. Mando doesn't say anything. He just walks right in, stands behind the official's son, raises his leg, and kicks." Tenoch bent his knee and made a kicking motion.

Suddenly, a burst of air assaulted the side of Wyler's face as the distinct sound of a suppressed gunshot broke the momentary silence. Red mist sprayed from Soto's forehead as a bullet ripped through it. Wyler flinched. He turned to see Soto's body sway for a second before toppling into the hungry mouth of the grave.

And just like that, Soto was dead.

It happened almost faster than Wyler's mind could process. One twitch of a finger, one tiny piece of metal flying at a couple thousand feet per second, was all it took to claim a life. The smell of cordite mixed with the metallic scent of blood. Wyler forced his head down despite the pain from the wire around his neck. He stared at Soto's lifeless body, contorted from the fall. Guilt uppercut Wyler in the gut. The voice in his head reassured him it wasn't his fault. It was Soto's choices that led them there, not his. The voice in Wyler's heart agreed. But despite all that, he still felt somehow to blame.

Tenoch stood and brushed the remnants of dirt from his hands. He stepped to the edge of the grave and peered down.

"The two dogs tore the official's son to pieces," Tenoch said. "His screams still come to me sometimes in my dreams. The official threw up. Puked right there. Collapsed in a ball of suffering."

Tenoch turned from the grave and walked to within a foot of Wyler. He crouched to be face-to-face.

"When the official finally stopped sobbing, Mando walked over to him and said, 'Are you ready to get to work?'" Tenoch grinned.

Wyler glared into the burning eyes. The urge to murder coursed through his veins. A driving palm to the nose would send bone into the man's brain...two thumbs to the eyes, gauging out those smoking embers...a violent twist of the head, breaking his neck. The fantasies rolled through Wyler's head like silent movies. But Soto's death wouldn't break him. It only served to feed the monster inside. He willed himself to survive no matter how long the odds were. Wyler hesitated only a moment before spitting in Tenoch's face.

"Hijo de puta," Tenoch said as he leaped back. He wiped the spit from his face with the back of his hand, then returned Wyler's gesture with one of his own. He kicked Wyler in the stomach with the heel of his boot. The strike knocked the air out of Wyler as he doubled over. Tenoch reared back and kicked Wyler in the ribs. Flashbulbs of red burst in his vision. Tenoch palmed the side of Wyler's head and smashed it into the ground. Keeping his hand in place, Tenoch dropped to his stomach, putting his face inches from Wyler's.

"You stubborn fucking mutt," Tenoch hissed.

Wyler smelled the tequila on his breath. The blaze in his eyes seared into Wyler's soul.

"I just had your fucking friend killed," Tenoch said. "And you're going to keep this shit up? And for what? Some dogs? Meaningless fucking creatures that no one will miss? Grow the fuck up."

With his free hand, Tenoch pulled out his handgun. He pressed the barrel against Wyler's forehead. "I should put a bullet right into that dimwitted brain of yours right now."

"T," Javier said.

Wyler sensed the nervousness in his voice. It told him he still wasn't meant to die yet.

"Shut up," Tenoch shouted at him. His gaze never left Wyler's. "I am those fucking dogs' God. I bring them into this world and choose how they leave it. I drown them. I slit their throats. I electrocute them. I bash their brains out with a hammer. Whatever the fuck I want. And sometimes I do it just because I can. It keeps them in their place. They bend to my will, and so will fucking you."

The barrel of the gun pressed harder into Wyler's forehead. Another twitch of a finger, and he'd be dead.

"T," Javier repeated. "Rafa said—"

"I know what he fucking said."

Wyler saw the debate raging over Tenoch's face like a storming ocean. For half a second, Wyler thought he would pull the trigger. But then the seas calmed, and his expression relaxed.

"No. Shooting you ... that would be too easy," Tenoch said. "I won't give you the satisfaction of a quick death." He used Wyler's head as leverage to push himself off the ground. "And I'm a man of my word. I said you had three chances. You've got one left."

Wyler lay there, catching his breath. A dull pain swelled through his chest. Possibly a cracked rib, he thought.

"Can't even kill me without your master's approval," Wyler said through clenched teeth. His blood was still hot from Soto's murder, and he couldn't stop himself from hurling one more dig at his tormentor. "Run along. I think I hear his whistle calling."

Tenoch's growl was the last thing Wyler heard before the butt of the gun struck him in the side of the head, hurtling him into the blackness once again.

Wyler drifted back to Atlantic City. The same memory as before, but four days later. It was a Saturday. He and the rescued Rottweiler—whom he named Maximus, based on Russell Crowe's character from *Gladiator*—walked underneath the Steel Pier. The dog kept tugging against his leash, desperately trying to get into the water. Wyler hesitated, fearing the dog would run away and never return. Like his first dog, Patches. He'd slipped out of his collar and took off straight into oncoming traffic. Time froze. The sound of screeching brakes and crunching bones haunted Wyler's dreams for months after the accident. A moment was all it took for the world to crumble. Aware of the loss's toll on their son, his parents reluctantly allowed him to keep the stray.

Wyler scanned the beach. They were alone.

"Alright, I'll let you go," Wyler said, crouching. He held up a stern finger to the dog. "But don't take off on me, and if any people come, don't bother them. Okay?"

Maximus licked Wyler's pointer and then tried playfully gnawing on it. Wyler laughed as he retracted his hand. "Alright, cut it out." Wyler unclipped the secondhand leash from the secondhand collar he bought from the Salvation Army. It had cut into his paltry savings, but he didn't care. For Maximus, he'd happily go broke.

When the leash came off, Maximus took a second to sniff the clip, then realizing he was free, bolted for the water. He slammed into a wave but kept going, unphased. Wyler laughed as the dog pranced through the sea like a deer. He found a small piece of driftwood and threw it into a swell, which Maximus chased down. They played fetch for nearly an hour. Time slipped by easily. Contentment filled his heart. All the other kids in his class wanted to play Playstation 2 all day, every day. But being on the beach, in the sun, with Maximus, was more than enough for Wyler. The simplicity of it didn't bother him in the slightest. Asking little from life, he found from a young age, was the only way to live.

As the sun began its descent, Wyler heard a voice that froze his blood.

"Look who we got here," the voice said.

Wyler spun to see the gang of four boys from the alleyway. They all wore similar cargo shorts with graphic t-shirts of New York sports teams or alternative bands like Linkin Park and System of a Down. The biggest kid was the one talking. Fresh scabs lined his wrists where Wyler had cut him with the bottle.

"That's our dog you've got there."

"He's not yours. Maximus, come here," Wyler shouted. He couldn't stop the panic in his voice. When the dog didn't immediately come to him, he shouted again, more frantic. "Maximus. Get over here."

"Maximus?" the biggest kid sneered. "Listen to this little bitch."

The other kids started laughing. Wyler waded into the ocean to wrangle the dog, but he kept darting away, thinking they were playing.

"Stop," Wyler shouted. His heart raced, and his breathing was bordering on hyperventilating. He dove at Maximus, fully submerging in the water. It drew more laughter from the kids. With one more lunge, Wyler managed to grab a hold of the dog's hind leg. Maximus yelped in pain. The sound sent a dagger into Wyler's chest, but it couldn't be avoided. He fumbled with the leash and finally got Maximus clipped in. When he turned around, the gang had closed in tight, surrounding him.

"Leave us alone," Wyler said, hating how pathetic and weak he sounded. Each time he spoke, he emboldened the gang. Wyler wrapped the leash around his hand multiple times to keep Maximus close.

"We'll leave you alone as soon as we get back what's ours," the biggest kid said.

"He's mine now," Wyler said, still unable to run.

And before Wyler could say anything else, one of the kids shoved him in the back. As he fell forward, the biggest kid twisted at the waist and rotated into his punch. Thick knuckles smashed into Wyler's chin. He felt like his entire jaw detached. When he crashed to the sand, the floodgates opened. Fists and feet hit him from every angle. Maximus barked and shuffled around, making it harder for Wyler to protect himself from the flurry of blows. The kids didn't laugh anymore as they carried out their work. Their young faces hardened into those of men. Each punch landed, knocked the innocence out of all of them. And what came next claimed a piece of their souls. The biggest kid barked an order, but Wyler couldn't hear it through the fuzzy static in his head. All he felt was a tugging on his arm before he passed out.

The incoming tide woke him a few minutes later. A quick scan told him the kids were gone. Wyler tasted blood. His head throbbed, and everything hurt. He looked down and noticed the leash was no longer around his hand. Panic forced him to his knees. The ground pitched as the blood rushed back to his head.

"Maximus," Wyler called. "Maximus."

He spun in a circle, looking for any signs of the gang or the dog. Then his gaze stopped on something ten yards away. A lump in the sand. His throat tightened, and all the moisture in his mouth evaporated. He forced his feet to move, knowing what the lump was.

"Maximus," Wyler whispered.

He fell to his knees in front of the dog's still body.

"Maximus?" Wyler whispered again as he gently shook the dog. "Are you okay, boy?"

He knew he wasn't. He knew the dog was dead. The pain in his heart drowned out all the pain in his body. Wyler scooped the dog into his arms and sat in the sand. As he stared at the darkening horizon beyond the ocean, he started to cry. It shocked him how quickly pure bliss could turn to utter misery. The idea of fairness was a joke that only a fool would believe in. Nothing was fair. When the tears stopped flowing, his chest heaved with the rhythm of the tide. And beneath his sadness, Wyler felt a twinge of something else inside his heart. Something he would spend the rest of his life fighting against from coming out and consuming him whole.

And that something was rage.

Pure, unfiltered rage.

Chapter 9

A fly landed on Wyler's dirt-caked face. His eyes opened to the harshness of a noon sun as he lay on his back. When he tried to swat the fly, his hand didn't move. He tilted his head to the right. Three feet of rope ran from his wrist to a stake in the ground. A quick scan revealed his other limbs were secured in the same fashion. Wyler squeezed his arms like he was on a butterfly press at the gym in an attempt to dislodge the stakes. After straining his muscles for ten seconds, he gave up. The stakes were driven in too deep. At first glance, his situation had gone from bad to worse. But he realized there was some good news as well.

The bad—that was pretty clear. Tenoch planned to leave him out in the sun to cook. When Wyler arrived yesterday, the temperature hit a high of a hundred and eighteen degrees. He could already feel the heat seeping into his skin. Sunburn would set in within fifteen minutes. Wyler didn't know Tenoch well, but he guessed the psycho wouldn't just leave him out there for fifteen minutes. An hour, maybe three at the most. They needed him alive still, didn't they? Or was that never actually the case? Had they planned to kill him regardless, and this was just their way of paying him back for busting them up, for not acquiescing? Based on the sun's location, Wyler gauged he could be exposed to the harmful rays for at least another seven hours. If they left him out there that entire time, his fried brain would either make him agree to anything or beg for a bullet to end his suffering. Neither were options Wyler looked forward to.

The good? No one was left behind to watch him, which presented an opportunity. Tenoch never mentioned anything about Blackjack, so the possibility remained that they hadn't caught him and he was still alive somewhere out in the desert. The other good thing was that the twins took Wyler's personal belongings, phone, wallet, watch, and knuckledusters, but they had overlooked his dog tags with the transmitter attached. The transmitter was his lifeline. His last chance for salvation. He felt the device resting against his chest. The only problem was he had to press the button to activate it. Without hands, that task wouldn't be easy, but it would not be impossible. At any rate, it was the only shot he had of walking out of the desert alive.

Wyler craned his head forward. He opened his mouth to get his chin to touch his chest. Then, he slowly worked it around until he felt the bumps of the chain. Using a twisting motion of his neck, he inched the chain up his chest. Sweat pooled on his forehead. Every second he took, the sun rose higher and burned hotter. Halfway through, his neck muscles spasmed, forcing him to throw his head back into the dirt. The dry air shriveled his lungs. He breathed heavily, wincing as the sinews in his neck went wild. After thirty seconds, the pain subsided. He rested another five minutes before the next effort.

His chin relocated the chain and tugged it a few more inches toward his left shoulder. When the transmitter got to his collarbone, Wyler rested his head again. For the next part, he had to proceed carefully. If the device slid over his shoulder and dropped down, he wasn't positive he'd be able to retrieve it. The sun continued to rise like a cannonball fired straight into the sky. The ground seemed to sizzle like hot oil in a skillet. With his right shoulder, Wyler wiped the sweat forming on his chin. He rested another minute, then went for the final push.

As the chain crept toward his shoulder, he focused on the slender object's location. It balanced in the divet of his collarbone. One wrong move and his chances of escape would plummet to zero. With the transmitter in place, Wyler twisted his neck and opened his mouth. His neck muscles screamed under the strain, but he ignored their pleas. Carefully, he put his mouth over the transmitter through his shirt. Using his tongue and teeth, he maneuvered the device until the button was vertical. A spasm ripped up his neck into the base of his skull. He wanted to shout but resisted the urge. With one last burst of effort, Wyler bit down on the device. He felt the button sink. Delicately, he opened his mouth, returning the transmitter to the valley of his collarbone. Craning his neck as far as he could, he stared at his shirt. The barely visible green glow winked through the fabric. The transmitter was armed.

Wyler dropped his head to the desert floor. He did all that he could do. Now, his fate rested on Blackjack. If a stranger had picked up the dog, Wyler was dead. If Blackjack was out of range, Wyler was dead. If the training hadn't stuck, he was dead, done, end of story. The transmitter had an advertised range of ten miles. As long as Blackjack hadn't traveled outside of that, there was hope, no matter how faint a glimmer.

Way up in the sky, Wyler spotted three specks circling. Hawks ... or vultures. For a second, Wyler felt like he was in an old Western movie. The sound of flies swarming reminded him he wasn't. He was in the real world, where he'd just witnessed his friend—or who he at least thought was his friend—get murdered. It was his dead body attracting the repulsive insects. Tenoch had staked Wyler a foot away from the grave. Scents of death and rot swept over him with the occasional breeze. The guilt grew in Wyler. He thought he'd known Soto, but maybe neither of them truly knew each other. Had he known the struggles Soto was going through sooner, maybe he could have done something. Avoided this whole mess from the start.

His mind drifted to Soto's parents. Wyler had met them once when he visited Soto in Los Angeles not long after they'd been discharged from the Marines. His parents welcomed Wyler into their home as if he was one of their own. They gave him food and beers, and they were nothing but warm. Now their son was dead, and Wyler's hands didn't feel clean. If he wound up in the grave with Soto, those same parents would never know what happened to their son. He'd have vanished without a trace, and every day, they'd be left wondering. Their grief would only be answered with silence. Wyler couldn't let that happen. He owed it to Soto and his parents. If he did that, then maybe, just maybe, he could repay his debt.

The vultures grew in size, having dropped slightly lower in the sky. Their faint screeches drifted down as they continued to circle. The sun was unrelenting. Wyler's clothes were soaked with sweat. His skin tingled as it headed past the sunburnt stage into second-degree burn territory. All the sweating combined with the heat made Wyler's mouth as dry as overcooked chicken. He closed his eyes and focused on his breathing. Four seconds on an inhale, followed by a four-second hold, then a four-second exhale, then another four-second hold. Repeat. It was another technique his ex, Enola, had taught him. She said it was a method Navy SEALS used. If it was good enough for one of the most elite military branches in the world, then it was good enough for him.

The thought of his ex shifted his focus to Ellie. He wondered how she'd react to him never returning. He pictured her playing it cool at first. She had a hard exterior and wouldn't allow her hurt to show. But then once a week turned into a month, he imagined the anger would set in. And what about after two months? Would she try to find him? He hadn't shared the darker parts of himself with her, so why would she think he'd possibly met a violent end instead of just being a jerk who ran off? The thought caused him a twinge of remorse for not being more open with her. All he could do, though, was change. If he survived, that was.

Wyler didn't believe in religion, so he wasn't about to start praying. He wouldn't do the cliché, 'Hey God, if you get me out of this jam, I'll change my ways.' No, fuck that, he thought. Ellie, Soto, and the dogs. They gave him all the reasons he needed to live. If wrongs needed to be righted, he would see them through to the very end. No matter what it took. No matter what it cost. He was going to survive. He was going to escape.

After fifteen minutes turned into fifty under the punishing sun, a touch of delirium plagued Wyler's mind. The buzzing of the flies seemed to intensify to the point where that was all he could hear. The sound was deafening, maddening. It conjured blurred snippets in his mind of what the noise signified: rotting flesh being devoured. He blinked repeatedly. Each time his eyes opened, though, he saw a mist of blood floating through the air. Don't crack, Wyler told himself. It's not real. Since keeping his eyes open wasn't doing him any good, he closed them and began to count. It gave him something simple to focus on and ground him in reality. He set a goal to count to ten minutes. Six hundred seconds. At three hundred, the sun felt like it was two inches from his body. He never hated the sun as much as he did at that moment. Keeping the count going got more challenging as his internal temperature rose. At five hundred, he drifted into a sort of twilight haze, where he was not fully awake and not fully asleep.

He hovered in that state until his subconscious slapped him awake. His eyes shot open. Wyler recognized the sensation on his right arm immediately—something crawling. It took every ounce of his willpower not to suddenly move to see what the insect was. Wyler held his breath as he slowly shifted his head to the right. Perched on his forearm was a scorpion. The flesh-colored bug stood out against Wyler's reddening skin. The scorpion stopped walking when Wyler looked at it as if it became aware of his presence. Wyler was no expert on the species but quickly decided the safest bet was to assume its sting was venomous.

With the bit of moisture left in Wyler's mouth, he whispered, "What do you say you give me a pass today, friend? I'm already a bit down on my luck." He chalked up talking to a scorpion as a sign of dehydration and the early onset of heat stroke.

The scorpion didn't move, and neither did Wyler. Time ceased to exist while he stared down the insect that could end him with one flick of its tail. Then, the scorpion moved a step, turning itself.

Wyler's heart felt like it might burst from his chest. As much as he didn't want to witness being stung, he didn't take his eyes off the scorpion. Another eternally long five seconds passed. Then the scorpion scurried off his forearm, darting toward his head. Wyler craned his neck as far as it would go, following the tiny creature's path. When it disappeared from his field of view, his body remained alert to any sensations of it crawling back on him somewhere else. Every muscle tensed. He'd read once that a scorpion sting could swell your throat, resulting in difficulty swallowing. The thought triggered Wyler to swallow. His throat was dry and swollen already. He couldn't imagine it getting even worse.

He quickly forgot about the insect when there was a sound of movement. Something larger approached. His mind raced to think of what other predators lurked in the desert. Coyotes, he thought, possibly mountain lions. Had the vultures landed? Or was it something worse? Tenoch? The twins? The only thing he could do was grit his teeth and await his fate.

Chapter 10

The movement stopped. Wyler held his breath, waiting. When no one spoke, and there were no sounds of a continued approach, Wyler counted to three, then raised his head. He prayed that what he saw wasn't a hallucination or a mirage.

Blackjack sat at his feet.

"Blackjack," Wyler whispered, close to tears. "What took you so long?"

Blackjack rushed forward and licked Wyler's face, whining slightly. The relief that flooded Wyler was only outdone by his pride for the dog.

"Okay, okay. Good boy," Wyler said. "Blackjack, sit."

Once he did, Wyler flicked his head, "Ropes. Bite. Go."

Blackjack hesitated. Wyler shook his hands, jiggling the ropes as he repeated the command. Blackjack moved to the mid-section of the rope attached to Wyler's right wrist.

"Bite."

Blackjack pawed at the rope, testing the resistance, then dove in. His teeth gnawed at the fibers.

"That's it. Good boy. Keep going. Bite."

Any pain Wyler felt vanished as he watched the dog working through the fibers.

"Almost there. Keep going."

As the rope frayed, Wyler tugged on it, weakening the connection further. Then, with one final burst of energy, he yanked, and the rope snapped. He laughed like an innocent death row inmate getting pardoned right before the needle entered his vein.

"That's how we do it."

Wyler ran his hand through Blackjack's fur, scratching him behind the ear.

"Good boy," Wyler said, rolling slightly to his left. He tapped the next rope. "Bite."

Blackjack did as instructed. Within minutes, his hands were free. When Wyler sat up, a tsunami of nausea sloshed through his gut. A tornado of dizziness cycloned around the walls of his skull. Roughly two hundred yards in the distance, the top half of Rafa's house protruded from the slight rise in the terrain, reminding him he wasn't out of the danger zone yet. He didn't know if someone was watching from the house. Over that distance someone could be on him in under five minutes. He fought through the sensations, overriding his battered body's protest and set Blackjack on the ropes binding his feet. While that was happening, Wyler unwove the knots at his wrists. The sweat dripping from his face evaporated almost as soon as it hit the dirt. From the wire bindings to the ropes, his wrists were torn to shit. He assessed his skin next. It was red and inflamed, but he didn't think it had gone past second-degree burns. In a few hours, though, Wyler knew he was going to be in ungodly pain. But that was a problem to deal with later. For now, he was just thankful to be alive and free. When Blackjack finished the final binding, Wyler removed the knots. Then he shifted stiffly to his knees and hugged Blackjack.

"Thank you," he whispered. "Thank you."

Wyler quickly inspected Blackjack for any injuries, constantly glancing from the dog to the house. His surface pass with his hands didn't turn up any physical issues. When he opened Blackjack's mouth, he saw the dog was just as dehydrated as himself. They needed to get out of the blistering sun. That became priority number one. Water was a close second. Third was not getting caught again. Staying low, he scanned the horizon in a three-hundred-and-sixty rotation. He gazed at the sun, orienting his location. A wall of mountains stretched behind him to the west. North and south showed more desert. East was civilization and safety.

He didn't know what other security Rafa or Tenoch might have protecting the surrounding property, so to minimize being seen, Wyler decided to go north and slightly to the west away from the house. The landscape left them exposed, but there was no way around it. If Tenoch didn't leave a man behind to bake in the heat with him, then he had to hope no one was watching from the house. It was possible they were overconfident he wouldn't be able to escape. Either way, he'd come too far to get careless. Once he felt they were far enough past the property, he would cut east toward the city.

"We've got a hike ahead of us," Wyler said. "You up for it?"

Blackjack barked once.

"Good boy."

Before leaving, Wyler peered into the grave. If it weren't for Blackjack, he'd have ended up in there. Soto's body had begun to swell from the heat. A foul stench hung in the air. Wyler didn't look away as he internalized a promise: *I'll come back for you. And I'll make them answer for what they've done. My debt will be paid.*

And then he set off into the desert.

Heat radiated off of every surface. The sun kept rising, dialing up the temperature. Wyler put it at over a hundred degrees with room to go. Every fifty yards, Wyler looked to the south, searching for signs of anyone chasing them. None appeared through the heat waves. After walking roughly half a mile, Blackjack's gait slowed as he limped slightly. Wyler stopped and inspected Blackjack's paws. Cracks lined his back pads. Blood oozed out of the rear right one. The terrain and heat were taking their toll. Blackjack's swollen tongue flopped out of his mouth. His breathing was heavy. Wyler knew they couldn't go much farther. They needed to cut east and get out of the sun. Wyler ripped off the sleeves of his shirt and tore them into four strips. He gently wrapped them around Blackjack's paws to provide minor protection against the scorching earth.

"Final push," Wyler said, rubbing Blackjack's side.

Wyler picked a spot on the horizon and navigated by it. Each step was an effort. His exposed skin continued to redden. To cut some of the monotony, Wyler established a routine of walking twenty steps, checking the horizon, ensuring Blackjack was still with him, then refocused on his compass point. Rinse and repeat. After the first mile, Wyler picked up on a patch of greenery against the sea of beige. He shielded his eyes from the sun and squinted into the distance. Almost positive he wasn't hallucinating, Wyler guessed he was staring at a golf course. That meant life. That meant water. That meant salvation.

"We're almost there."

When he looked back, Blackjack was lying on the ground, panting.

"We can't quit now. Come on."

Wyler crouched and scooped the dog into his arms. Blackjack groaned when Wyler stumbled as he adjusted to carrying the weight. The fur chafed against Wyler's sunburnt skin, but he ignored the pain. At this point, giving up wasn't an option. There was still too much work to be done. After a few steps, Wyler found his footing. He staggered forward. Keep going, he told himself; don't stop. The terrain pitched slightly, propelling Wyler's momentum. A hundred yards remained. The greenness of the grass beckoned to him. His legs switched to autopilot. Five yards from the green, the ground rose on a gradual slope. Wyler dug deep and propelled them over the lip. He dropped to his knees and lowered Blackjack to his feet. After the bleakness of the desert, the grass beneath him felt like he'd landed on a lush hillside in Ireland.

While Wyler caught his breath, he looked around. A foursome was setting up on the tee five hundred yards back. To his right, twenty yards off, was the next hole's empty tee area. A sculpted box rested on a four-legged platform. His heart skipped a beat when he realized what it was.

"Come on," Wyler said. He pushed to his feet and headed for the box. When he got in front of it, he found the spigot. He crouched and twisted the lever. Ice-cold water poured from the spout. He chugged the water but was careful not to overdo it. His mind flooded with ecstasy. After dunking his head under the water, he grabbed a paper cup from the sleeve attached to the side. He filled it and held it for Blackjack to drink from. Blackjack lapped up the water in seconds. Ten cups later, Blackjack's thirst was quenched. Wyler dumped two full cups on Blackjack's head, then soaked the makeshift bandages around his paws.

After one more drink, they set off for a walking path to the side of the tee. It took them ten minutes to find their way to the clubhouse. When Wyler saw it, he stopped. They weren't safe yet, and his appearance, he knew, was sure to draw some looks and possibly questions. If he played things wrong now, and someone justifiably thought he was insane, the cops could get called. And from what Soto told him, Rafa and Agosti had police on their payroll. It was possible for Wyler to get an honest cop to take him in, but it wasn't a chance he was willing to take. For all he knew, the cops would show up, take one look at him, and open fire. No. The cops weren't an ideal first step. Getting back to the hotel, grabbing his gear and the Bronco, he determined was the better route.

The hotel was at least five miles away. Neither he nor Blackjack were in any shape for a trek like that on foot. Plus, it would cost them more time. Wyler didn't know how long it would take Tenoch to discover him gone. But once that happened, Wyler guessed people would come after him. He was still a liability. So, every second mattered.

Wyler circled behind the clubhouse, trying to act casual and not draw attention to himself. At the back, he spotted a row of golf carts. It was a good forty yards away from the first tee. A white kid with a buzz cut, maybe sixteen or seventeen, dressed in khaki shorts and a tucked-in red polo shirt, was wiping down the electric vehicles with a towel. The way the kid worked, quiet and eager with a look that said, 'The world hasn't disillusioned me yet,' gave Wyler an idea.

He bent down, untied his left shoe, and pried it off. Then he rolled down his sock and peeled off the folded five hundred dollars stuck to the top of his foot. The bills were saturated with sweat but still intact. *No one checks the socks.* His father's words echoed through his mind. Wyler shook his head with a grin, remembering his old man, while he put his shoe back on. He repeated the process with his other foot, then unfolded the cash and stuffed it in his pockets.

"Stay," Wyler said to Blackjack. "I'll be right back."

Wyler scanned the area. Not seeing anyone else, he went for it. When Wyler reached the end of the line of carts, he slowed down. The kid was occupied with his menial task and didn't notice Wyler's approach.

"Hello," Wyler said in a friendly, non-threatening, non-lunatic voice.

The kid turned with a smile that vanished instantly when his focus landed on Wyler.

"Hi, sorry to bother you," Wyler said. He held out his hands, spreading his fingers like he was trying to steady a spooked horse.

"Uh, hi," the kid said. "Can I ... can I help you?"

"I know I look a bit wild," Wyler said, turning on a disarming smile. "I was at my buddy's bachelor party last night, and needless to say, things got out of hand."

The kid glanced toward the clubhouse. Probably searching for an adult to scream to if the dirty, burnt, sleeveless guy in front of him tried anything, Wyler thought.

"Okay?" the kid said.

"I know this will sound crazy, but I lost my phone, watch, and everything else. Do you have a phone?"

The kid nodded. "Do you need me to call you a doctor?"

"No. That's alright, thank you. What I could use, though, is a ride." Wyler held out one of the hundred dollar bills. "I'll pay you a hundred dollars if you can order me a taxi, Uber, Lyft... whatever is around here."

"You'll give me a hundred bucks for that? That's it?"

"That's it," Wyler said. "And there's another hundred in it for you if you keep this between me and you."

The kid narrowed his eyes. Wyler thought for a second he overplayed it with the last part, and the kid was going to bolt. But he didn't. The kid shrugged and took out his phone.

"Alright, if that's all you need, I can do that. We have a setup with Lyft. Usually, though, we use that for our members that drink too much in the clubhouse." The kid typed away on his phone. Wyler released a breath, feeling a slight breeze of luck passing back in his direction.

"What's your name?"

"You can put down Ethan," Wyler said, giving the kid one of his aliases.

"And where are you going?"

"JW Marriott in Sumerlin."

"Okay," the kid said, continuing to tap away. "You're all set." He pointed toward where Wyler had come from. "They'll pick you up front over there."

"How do I know it's them?

The kid tugged on his red polo shirt. "They'll have a sign on the dashboard that's this color with the course's logo printed on it."

"Easy enough. Hey, listen, I appreciate it, kid." Wyler plucked another hundred from the sweaty clump and held the two bills out. The kid frowned at the saturated state of the money.

"Did you fall into a pool or something, too?" the kid said, using his thumb and index finger like tweezers to take the soggy cash.

"Yeah," Wyler said, not having the heart to tell him it was foot sweat. "Like I said, it was a crazy night."

"Well ..." the kid laid the hundreds on a white towel to dry. "Thanks."

"The thanks are all mine. Take it easy."

Wyler collected Blackjack and went to wait for the driver, lingering off the side of the main entrance near a palm tree. He caught a couple of double-take glances from the stuffy wealthy patrons heading in for a round of eighteen. But no one stopped to ask what his deal was, which he figured was understandable. Twenty-five minutes later, a black 2018 Chrysler 300 with a red sign on the dash pulled to the curb in front of the clubhouse. Initially, the driver refused to let Blackjack in the car, but he relented after Wyler offered up another two hundred dollars to cover any cleaning costs. As the air conditioning washed over him, the thought that he'd just spent four hundred dollars on a ten-minute car ride drifted away.

When the car stopped at the hotel, Wyler entered a sea of activity. Leaving guests handed over their valet tickets while others stood near their luggage waiting for their vehicles to arrive. Cars moved through the roundabout with an orchestrated fluidity. Wyler scanned the area for any potential dangers. Seeing none, he let Blackjack out, then forked over the two hundred dollars to the driver, who accepted the wet bills with the same look of skepticism as the kid at the golf course. They'd get over it, he knew. Money had a way of cleansing the memory of any negative thoughts associated with it.

Wyler walked up to the front desk. The same concierge, Dawn, he'd met less than twenty-four hours ago greeted him with a forced tight-lip smile. It was another stroke of luck that she was there, Wyler thought, since Tenoch had stripped him of his wallet and any proof of who he was. His current physical condition didn't make him the poster child of believability that he was a guest at such a ritzy hotel.

"My … it looks like someone had an eventful evening," Dawn said.

Wyler grinned. "It was so eventful, I seemed to have misplaced my room key."

She arched her eyebrows in a way that said, 'Say no more; I've seen this before.' Her fingers flew across the keyboard. Then she leaned over and produced a fresh keycard from a drawer.

"Anything else I can help you with?" she said, handing him the thin plastic card. "An appointment at our spa, perhaps?"

"I'll take a raincheck on that."

"Alright. If you change your mind, I'm just a phone call away. Enjoy the rest of your day."

The elevator opened, and Wyler and Blackjack headed for their room. Once inside, Wyler quickly washed the dirt and sweat off his face in the bathroom sink. He desperately needed a shower but didn't want to stick around any longer than he needed to. It would have to wait. Instead, he soaked a washcloth in freezing water and dabbed it against his arms and neck, wiping away as much of the desert as possible. His skin was headed toward a deep maroon color. No stranger to sunburns, he knew the pain would kick in soon. It would be a long two or three days before the worst of it was over. He'd deal with that as it came. Now, he needed to keep moving.

He left the bathroom, grabbed his bag, and pulled out fresh

clothes. His skin screamed as he peeled off the remnants of his shirt. He pushed past the burning sensation and finished getting dressed. With the dirt off and new threads on, Wyler felt better, recharging like a battery on empty. As Wyler finished zipping his bag, Blackjack jerked his head toward the door. His body stiffened as he got to his feet and crept forward in an attack crouch. Wyler recognized the signs—a threat was detected. He didn't yet know the specifics of what Blackjack sensed or heard. That was the way it went. Blackjack served as an early alert system, leaving Wyler to react to whatever presented itself.

Wyler fell in line behind the dog as he continued toward the door. Then, there was a beep and an electric grinding as the lock released. Blackjack stopped. Wyler froze. His pulse quickened, and his fingers curled into fists. Please just be housekeeping, he thought. The door edged open slowly. The kind of slow that doesn't want to make any noise. Not the way housekeeping would open the door. Then, the appearance of a gun suppressor peeked through the crack.

Chapter 11

Close-quarter combat always reminded Wyler of being on one of those slingshot amusement park rides. Time seemed to freeze in anticipation of the release. Then, in a split second, you left the world behind at a hundred miles an hour. Everything whipped past in a blur with your stomach at your toes, barely able to breathe. And as the silenced gun came further into the room, Wyler's instincts took over and he left the world behind.

His shoulder slammed into the door, smashing it against the unknown assailant's wrists. A shout followed as the gun clanked to the floor. Wyler kept going. He yanked on the handle. The Scorpion-tattooed twin, Javier, stood in the hallway, clutching his wrist. Seeing him there caught Wyler momentarily by surprise. He at least knew now that Tenoch had discovered him missing.

Javier gave up massaging his wrist and went for something behind his back as he released an angry snarl. Wyler rushed him before he could reach whatever it was. They slammed into the adjacent wall. The sheetrock groaned as they nearly went through it. Javier countered with a headbutt. A high-pitched echo rattled through Wyler's head as the blow connected with his right eye socket. A burst of white light exploded across his vision. Javier shifted his weight and used his foot to push off the wall, sending them careening back into Wyler's room. For someone on the smaller side, the guy had more strength than Wyler anticipated. Blackjack immediately entered the fray, snapping at Javier's legs. His jaws caught fabric but not flesh. The three of them grappled in the tight quarters of the foyer, bouncing off the walls, each fighting for their lives.

A quick jab landed in Wyler's ribs, sending a whoosh of air from his lungs. The shooting pain loosened his grip. Javier then shot both of his elbows down into Wyler's forearms, breaking their grapple. With his arms free, he shoved Wyler back. The small gap of separation allowed him to focus on Blackjack. He took one step, forcing the dog into the bathroom. With his other leg, Javier lashed out at Blackjack's face. Seeing the blow coming, Blackjack released his hold on the pants, dodging the strike by centimeters. Javier grabbed the handle before Blackjack could gain traction on the slick tiled floor and slammed the door shut.

Fueled by a rising rage, Wyler ran at Javier. He skidded to a stop halfway there when Javier whipped a folding knife from his back pocket and flicked it open. Wyler slowly backpedaled into the bedroom with more space to maneuver. His eyes darted around, looking for anything he could use as a weapon. Blackjack barked from the bathroom and frantically clawed at the door. To Wyler, the noise was like hearing a baby cry. It did something to him inside. It made him want to do bad things.

Javier grinned as he rolled his shoulders, readying to attack. Wyler glanced to his right. His belt sat at the top of his bag. It wasn't an ideal choice against a knife, but it was better than nothing. He quickly reached out and snatched it. Seeing the belt made Javier's grin widen. Wyler got the impression the man enjoyed murder. Javier closed the distance to eight feet. Wyler passed the large cabinet that doubled as a dresser on one side and a TV stand on the other. He studied Javier's eyes. He found people's eyes usually narrowed ever so slightly right before any sudden movements. As Wyler kept backpedaling, he threaded the tail end of the belt through the buckle, creating a loop. Blackjack continued to bark. The sound mixed with Wyler's thumping heart created a steady beat in his ears. His muscles were tense, ready for anything. And then the attack came.

Javier rushed forward, raising the knife high with a feral growl. Wyler waited until the last possible second before making his move. He shot his left hand out and swiped open the dresser's top drawer. Javier started to spin to avoid it, but he was going too fast. The drawer connected where his groin met his thigh, eliciting a grunt. He pitched forward, naturally putting his hands out to break his fall. Wyler dashed to the right and leaped onto the bed to get the height he needed. The springs screeched under his weight. Without stopping, he looped the belt over Javier's head, seating it around his neck as he launched himself off the bed like a TV wrestler, kicking his feet out horizontally so he would land on his ass. Wyler hit the floor with a heavy thump. The downward force jerked Javier's head back violently. Wyler cinched the belt tightly and pulled with all of his might. Javier took one desperate swipe with his knife that missed Wyler by a mile. He quickly abandoned the knife as his oxygen supply rapidly dwindled. His fingers clawed at the belt, as a sickening wheeze gurgled from his throat.

Escape was futile for Javier. The rage that Wyler worked hard to keep caged overran his defenses. He pictured the bullet hole in Soto's face. He heard the sound of the buzzing flies. He saw the circling buzzards waiting to feast. This man had killed his friend. This man was involved with people who hurt dogs. An image of the dead and drowned Maximus then materialized in Wyler's rage-induced mind. He pulled the belt even tighter. The rage drowned out protests from the voices of reason in his head and heart. No, Wyler knew this man was going to die. He grit his teeth and kept the tension on the belt. Within twenty seconds, Javier's fight slowed. The wheezing faded to a wet bubbling sound. After forty seconds, his hands went limp and dropped to the floor. But Wyler didn't release the pressure. He kept squeezing well past the point that anyone could survive without oxygen.

Only then did the voice of reason in his head break through the rage. It told him Javier was dead. Slowly, Wyler released his hold on the belt. He slid out from underneath the body and then felt for a pulse. Nothing. Another life claimed. Wyler stood and caught his breath while the adrenaline began its retreat. Looking at the body didn't stir any remorse in Wyler. Only a twinge of guilt. But not guilt because he killed someone, guilt for not feeling bad about it.

And that's when he thought of Ellie. This was the part of himself that he feared revealing to her. How could she love someone who felt nothing staring at a corpse? To love him, in part, was to love a monster. Ellie deserved better, didn't she? Or was that not for him to decide? Then Wyler thought of his ex, Enola. They drifted apart because she wanted to focus on her work.

But maybe ... maybe she saw who he really was deep inside, so she pushed him away. Would the same thing happen with Ellie?

Blackjack barked again, snapping Wyler from his philosophical ponderings. He shook his head and came back to the moment.

Wyler let Blackjack out of the bathroom, then found the gun Javier had dropped. It was a Springfield Armory Hellcat. A rugged, compact carry gun. Wyler ejected the magazine and noted it held fourteen rounds. He reinserted it and then checked the breach. A round was in the chamber, ready to fire. Wyler peered through the peephole on the door. He didn't see anyone, but that didn't mean Javier hadn't come with backup.

"On me," Wyler said to Blackjack. He held his breath, and with the gun at the ready, he opened the door leading into the hallway. "Search."

Blackjack darted out. Wyler watched for a second while Blackjack went left, then he looked right. No one was there. It took Blackjack under two minutes to clear the floor. Once he did, they went back into the room. Wyler threw the latch, and then removed the suppressor from the barrel of the gun, making it easier to holster it at his hip. Things were moving too fast. He needed time to consider his options and what he would do next. Wyler sat on the couch, closed his eyes, and started a breathing routine. Slow the mind. Slow the heart. Focus. Rescuing the pit bulls topped his list, and on the car ride to the hotel, he had worked out a rough idea of how he could do it.

The issue that faced him, though, was time. Javier showing up meant Tenoch knew Wyler escaped and was a huge liability. If Wyler wasn't found, Tenoch and Rafa would have a decision to make. Do they move the dogs, or worse, kill them, to destroy evidence should law enforcement not on Rafa's payroll show up?

Or did they take their chances and do nothing differently while they continued to look for Wyler? From what he knew of Rafa's situation, it seemed unlikely they would move the dogs. That would require time, which Rafa also didn't sound to have a lot of from what Soto outlined. That left them the option of either disposing of the evidence or doing nothing. Again, killing the dogs seemed unlikely to Wyler. Rafa's entire future business rode on the backs of those dogs. If they were gone, he risked losing the fight, bet, and land deal.

Wyler stood and paced the living room. If his assumptions were correct, where did that leave him? What would Rafa and Tenoch assume Wyler would do next? Most people in the same situation would count their lucky stars, get out of the city as fast as possible, and pray they never saw Tenoch again. Others might try the cops. Wyler doubted Tenoch or Rafa would expect him to return for the dogs, which created the advantage of surprise. But that would only get him so far. To pull off the plan percolating in Wyler's mind, he needed his enemies gone from the house long enough to get the dogs. It was a challenge, but not an impossible one to overcome. And he knew just the person to reach out to for help. That would also have to wait, Wyler thought as he watched Blackjack sniff the dead body. More pressing issues faced him in the present.

No one else attempted to enter the room. Wyler interpreted that fact to mean Javier came alone or someone drove and waited outside. Regardless, the body was an issue. Wyler's real name was tied to the room. When Javier was discovered, the police would put Wyler at the top of the suspect list. And as far as he was concerned, he didn't want anyone else looking for him. But what was he going to do with the body? Wyler rubbed his chin while he scanned the room. His gaze stopped on the balcony, and an idea washed over him all at once. It wasn't a pretty solution, but it was an effective one.

He opened the doors and walked into the heat. The five o'clock sun lined distant mountains with shadows. Sounds of nature and life carrying on murmured beneath him. He went to the railing and looked down. The walkways below were deserted, as were the other balconies lining the face of the hotel. No guests and no cameras that he could spot. Both good signs. Wyler looked down again, gauging distances. The fourth-floor height would do a good enough job masking how Javier was killed. Wyler knew a full-blown autopsy would reveal Javier was strangled. The solution wasn't perfect, but it would buy Wyler time and distance himself from being a suspect. He banked on investigators struggling to pinpoint the specific room Javier 'jumped' from.

Wyler stepped back into the room and crouched beside Javier. He emptied the man's pockets, producing a wallet, phone, keys, lighter, and a spare ammo magazine. Wyler shoved the objects into his pockets, wanting to remove all identification. Anything to make it harder for the cops to ID the body played in Wyler's favor. It also meant Tenoch wouldn't know what happened to Javier for longer.

Wyler did another sweep of the room, ensuring he left nothing behind. Satisfied, he got to work with the more grisly business at hand. He looped his arms under Javier's and dragged him to the balcony. A subtle putrid scent of death wafted to his nose. He took a breath, readying himself for the last part. There could be no hesitation. He needed to go as fast as he could. Wyler bent down and scooped Javier into his arms like a sleeping child. His knees strained as he forced himself to a standing position.

Then he shuffled forward, cleared Javier's feet of the railing, then shoved. The body plummeted ungracefully through the air, then hit the walkway with a muffled thump. The sight still stirred nothing inside Wyler. He lingered on the corpse for one last dispassionate second before he darted back into the room, grabbed his bag, and headed for the door.

His pulse quickened as he entered the hallway. He figured he had ten minutes tops before someone found the body, then maybe another ten before the cops showed up. He wanted to be long gone by that time.

"Stay close," Wyler said to Blackjack. His partner dutifully carried on alongside him, but Wyler noticed his limp worsening. "Just a little longer, then I'll get you fixed up properly."

They got on the elevator and rode it down. In the lobby, Wyler continually scanned for Tenoch, Xolo, or anyone else who seemed off. Outside, Wyler approached the valet station and handed over his ticket. Once the valet left, Wyler moved behind a large column supporting the entrance overhang. Staying out of sight, he kept watch for anyone approaching. Time seemed like it was stuck in a Scottish bog. Wyler rested his hand near the butt of the gun. It reassured him and eased some of the tension of his frayed nerves.

Then he heard the scream. His heart raced, pressing against his bruised ribs. Things were about to start happening. He willed the valet to appear with the Bronco.

"Come on," he said under his breath.

More screams. The other guests, waiting for their cars, looked around, alarmed, unsure of what was happening. Two people dressed in hotel uniforms ran through the entrance.

How long does it take to get one goddamn car, Wyler thought?

The countdown clock started in Wyler's head. His original assessment of ten minutes for the cops to arrive was flawed. He didn't take into account the wealth of the area. For the rich and powerful, the cops didn't waste time. Then, the sound of the first siren came. It was closer than he wanted. Three minutes tops, and they'd be there. Movement to his left caught his eye. The Bronco. He'd never been more happy to see a vehicle in his life. When the valet stopped, Wyler ditched his post and hustled to the passenger door. He let Blackjack in, then tossed the bag on the floor. At the driver's door, he gave the valet another sweaty hundred-dollar bill, then jumped in. He threw the car into drive and hit the gas. The Bronco ripped through the roundabout onto the two-lane road divided by a string of palm trees. He skidded to a halt at a four-way intersection. Flashing lights were coming in the opposite direction. Wyler turned right. His eyes glued to the rearview mirror, watching as an ambulance and two cop cars streaked past. None of them came after him. He exhaled, then turned left onto Rampart Blvd., stepped on the throttle, and didn't look back.

PART

2

Chapter 12

Detective Joel Amos parked the unmarked Dodge Charger in the front lot of the JW Marriott hotel. He pulled a four-and-a-half-inch Kent comb from the inside pocket of his ash-colored tailored suit. His hair was the shade of black tea and was sculpted to perfection, with the sides and back buzzed close in a clean fade. He ran the comb through his hair with short, practiced strokes, six to be precise, three in the front, three in the back. A glance in the rearview confirmed every follicle was where it was supposed to be. After tucking the comb back inside his jacket, he exited the car. In the reflection of the driver's window, Amos fixed the knot of his tie.

Appearances mattered to him. His face was that of a B-list movie star. They got him by with the fairer sex. But whatever he lacked in the looks department he made up for with confidence and an air of authority. That was what really drew people to him. And the clothes and the hair were part of the persona he projected into the world. His days were varied and often met with a selection of people from a range of social classes. One minute, he could be telling a mother her kid had been killed; in another, he could be talking with a local official about the state of crime in the community. People looked to him for answers of one kind or another. And no one wanted to get answers from a slob. The first five seconds of meeting someone said a lot. For Amos, he wanted those five seconds to say, 'You can trust me,' especially when he crossed the lines cops weren't supposed to cross. Appearances mattered.

Amos adjusted the Glock on his hip, then slipped a Listerine sheet onto his tongue. He liked the tingling sensation. It meant the sheet was doing its job. Fresh breath, just one more piece of the persona. He walked out of the lot and up the driveway. Two uniformed cops stood near the entrance, bullshiting. Amos tossed them his signature half smile while he flashed his badge.

"Heard we got a jumper," Amos said.

The cop on the left, a young Asian guy, barely looked at the badge and nodded. "Yeah, that's what dispatch said anyway."

Amos noted the cop's name from the rectangle clip on his chest. "Anyone on the scene yet, Chan?" He liked to call people by their names. It was a subtle technique, but he found it worked to create a quick connection with whoever he was talking to. Especially cops. It made them feel seen instead of being some disposable grunt.

"Yeah. Cameron's back there."

"One of you mind taking me over?"

"Sure," Chan said. "Come on."

Chan led him through the hotel's posh lobby to a rear entrance, where more cops stood guard. The doors led to a small enclave hemmed in by three sides of the sprawling hotel.

"Thanks, Chan," Amos said, tossing him a curt wave goodbye.

A group huddled loosely on a path fifteen yards away. Two in the group were from forensics, snapping photos at the ground. Amos hadn't seen the body yet, but he had a good idea where it was. Elijah Cameron was hovering over one of the lab guy's shoulder, scribbling furiously in a notepad. Of all the detectives to get the case, Amos thought, why'd it have to be Cameron? The guy was a Holy Crusader who followed the letter of the law literally, often citing passages from the rulebook verbatim whenever someone suggested a questionable solution to a problem. Amos and his buddies would do their best impersonation over beers. It was comedic gold. But for this particular case, Amos wasn't laughing.

He strolled down the path, looking up at the rooms for possible jumping locations. The hotel wasn't that tall, so wherever the guy came from, it had to be one of the top floors to do any real damage. Then again, Amos had a case where a person died after being shoved down five steps. The Bishops. A husband and wife dispute. Wife shoved, husband fell, hit his head on the basement floor just right, and it was lights out. She got sent up for a five-year manslaughter stint.

"Looks like someone mistook the balcony for a diving board," Amos said as he approached.

Cameron jerked his head back and scowled when he spotted Amos.

"Real fucking classy," Cameron said. They shared their disdain for one another.

"Classy is my middle name."

"What are you doing here, Amos?"

"That's a dead body, and the last I checked, I was a homicide detective."

Cameron snorted. "That's rich." He returned his attention to the victim.

Cameron's partner, Jim Hobart, came over and shook Amos's hand. "Amos."

"How you doing, Jim?"

"Just trying to make it to retirement without shoveling too much shit off the sidewalk, but ..." He nodded toward the body, "... here we are."

Amos crouched, studying the corpse. A pool of dried blood caked the pink cement beneath his head. The victim's right arm was bent in the wrong direction.

"We know what room he was in?" Amos said to Hobart over his shoulder as his eyes moved to the distinct tattoo of a scorpion tail wrapped around the victim's neck.

"No," Hobart said. "There's no ID on him. Don't know who the hell he is yet. We'll take some prints and see if he comes up in the system."

His name was Javier Herrera, Amos wanted to say. He knew the corpse. But he wasn't about to share that with Hobart or Cameron. Amos nodded, careful not to put any recognition on his face. An EMT and another cop lingered off to the side watching. As Amos stood, he made a second of eye contact with the cop, Bergman. He was a like-minded individual who worked with the same off-the-books people Amos did. Bergman was the one who tipped off Amos to come to the scene. The kid was smart to do so.

"What do you think?" Hobart said. "Another poor soul that blew his life savings on the tables? Decided a swan dive would solve his problems?"

Amos shrugged. Before he could say anything, Cameron chimed in.

"I don't like it. No offense, but this guy doesn't look like the normal clientele that stays here. He looks like a gang banger to me. They got their own places to gamble."

"Aside from your not-so-subtle racism," Amos said. "What are you suggesting? You think one of these rich yuppies offed him?" Amos wanted to hear Cameron's line of thinking. The more he knew, the easier it would be to handle whatever situation was brewing.

"Hey, nothing is off the table at this point," Cameron said, staring at Amos. "If money's involved, people are liable to do bad things. You should know that better than anybody."

Amos grinned at the dig. He knew about the whispers amongst the straight-edge cops that he was possibly dirty. But he didn't care. Let them gossip. He'd taken precautions every time he'd crossed the line. Anything Cameron or anyone else thought they had was pure speculation. In their line of work, proof was the only thing that mattered, and Cameron had none of it.

"I feel there's an accusation in there," Amos said.

"Tell me why you're here."

"Guys, please," Hobart said, holding out his hands like a referee, sensing where the conversation was going. "We're all adults here. Let's act like it, huh? We've got plenty of witnesses to talk to while we find out who the hell this guy is. Come on, Cameron, let's go. Cool off. And you ..." Hobart said, pointing at Amos, "... don't fuck up our crime scene."

Amos held out his hands with a 'who me?' face. "I agree with you, Jim. This guy probably couldn't handle a losing streak and took the easy way out. My bet is this isn't even a crime scene."

Hobart laughed cynically as he put his hand on Cameron's arm to lead him inside the hotel.

"You think we'd get that fucking lucky?" Hobart said.

"A man makes his own luck."

"Jesus," Cameron groaned. "Save that shit for the tourists."

Once Cameron and Hobart disappeared inside, Amos gave Bergman a nod of gratitude, then walked away from the body. He strolled into a parking lot with a view of part of the golf course. He looked around to ensure no one was watching him before removing his secondary phone from his suit jacket. After a deep breath, he placed the call.

Tenoch answered on the fourth ring.

"What have you got?" he said.

The voice was as cold and intense as when Amos met him in Los Angeles. Amos had been on the job for four years at that point. He busted his ass, working in some of the toughest neighborhoods to make a name for himself. Forward thinking. That was the motto that he lived by. Do the hard work and ascend the ranks. He had his sights set on becoming one of the youngest chiefs in the history of the LAPD. And after that, maybe he'd branch out into government. Senator Amos had a nice ring to it, he thought. The sky was the limit. But after getting passed over three times for promotions due to politics and affirmative action, he developed a chip on his shoulder. That chip opened into a chasm of resentment. Why was he working so hard for so little reward? The question began to eat away at him.

Then he met Tenoch. Amos had pulled him over in an area known for drug trafficking. And sure enough, in the trunk of his car were four bricks of cocaine. Most guys in Tenoch's situation either made a break for it or tried to bribe their way free. Tenoch took the second approach but did it in a way unlike any other lowlife had done before.

Tenoch had said, "Think of me like a genie. You let me leave here; I'll turn that powder in the back into one wish for you."

The proposition amused Amos at first. But the fire that burned in Tenoch's eyes told Amos this guy was different. Those eyes promised opportunity. Amos rationalized that even if he arrested Tenoch, more drugs would find their way onto the streets, so why not let him go and see what happened?

"Get me onto one of the major crimes divisions," Amos said. "Otherwise, I'll track you down with a SWAT team in tow and make sure you do at least twenty in San Quentin."

Tenoch grinned. "Your wish is granted."

A month later, Amos got onto the Gang and Narcotics Division with a raise and a title bump. How Tenoch pulled it off, Amos could only imagine. But that was the start of a decades long partnership. And when Tenoch shipped off to Vegas to blaze a new frontier, Amos followed.

"Can you talk?" Amos asked.

A brief pause followed, and then Tenoch said, "Alright, go ahead."

"It's about your man, Javier."

"What about him?"

"He's dead."

Another pause. "Where?"

"At the JW Marriott. A guest found him flattened out on a walkway in an apparent suicide."

"Hijo de puta," Tenoch cursed. "Suicide?"

"Looking like he jumped out of a window."

"Mother fucker."

"Did you know he was here?"

"Yeah. It was one place he was supposed to check."

"Check for what?"

Tenoch paused again.

"What's going on?" Amos said.

Tenoch let out a heavy sigh, then filled Amos in on what happened with Wyler.

"Fuck," Amos said once Tenoch finished. "So you think this guy ... Wyler ... you think he killed Javier?"

"He sure as fuck didn't jump out of a goddamn window."

"Alright."

"I need you to work this. We need this guy to go away. You know what's on the line."

Amos did. The bet and the land deal. The dog fights were only a month away. Amos thought they were a bad idea and told Tenoch as much, but it ultimately wasn't his decision. He conceded if it ended the feuding and bodies showing up on streets, then that was something at least. Amos understood what he stood to gain, being on the winning side of the land deal. It meant more wealth for Rafa and Tenoch, which meant more money could be funneled towards Amos's campaigns for police chief then one day congress.

"I can handle it," Amos said. "There's already two detectives on the case, but I can work around them. What else do you know about this guy I'm looking for? Any other ideas where he might have gone?"

"I only knew about the hotel. He's originally from New Jersey."

"Okay. That's good. Anything else? Doesn't matter how small

it is."

"Fuck, I don't know," Tenoch said. "He was military. Some sort of hard ass who did tours overseas. Trains dogs … and he's got a dog with him."

"A dog?"

"That's right."

"What kind?"

"A Belgian Malinois."

"Sounds fancy."

"It looks like a slightly smaller German Shepherd."

"Got it," Amos said. He scanned the parking lot, confirming he was still alone. "What about his car? What's he driving?"

"No clue."

There wasn't much to go on, but Amos never avoided a challenge. He prided himself on his resourcefulness.

"And if I find him …" Amos said.

"If you find him, put a bullet in his fucking head. He's useless to us, and we can't take the chance on him talking to anyone we don't control."

Amos had fired his gun on six different occasions while on the job in LA. He'd taken two lives, one a drug dealer and one a lowlife coming out of a convenience store during a robbery. They were both clean shootings, and he was cleared in each. But he'd yet to take a life for Tenoch. Did he help cover up murders on his behalf? Sure. Dispose of evidence? Yes. Lead investigations away from their dealings? Yes again. Killing, though, brought new risks and a life sentence if he got caught. The rewards, though, were also greater. Taking care of a problem of this magnitude would buy him even more security within the organization. His ticket to bigger and better things would be all but punched.

"Alright," Amos said. "I'll keep you updated. If anything changes on your end, let me know."

Tenoch hung up. Amos tucked the phone back into his pocket and removed his comb. He ran it through his hair again. His day had just gotten a lot more interesting.

Amos leaned against the concierge counter and flashed his badge.

"Hi there, Dawn," he said to the concierge. "Detective Amos. I was hoping you could help me access a guest's room."

"Does this have to do with ... what happened out there?" Dawn said, nodding toward the door.

"It is."

"Can I ask what exactly happened?"

The concierge sat up straighter in her chair, eager for the chance to be involved. TV and movies had done a number on the profession, Amos thought. Death and the uglier parts of humanity were mainstream now. It was easy for people's fascinations to grow from a distance, sitting in the safety of their homes or listening to podcasts in their cars. If the crimes touched their own lives, though, it became a different story. He'd seen a lot of faces sobered by reality, shocked that the brutality they usually delighted in had happened to them.

"I shouldn't be discussing this," Amos said, lowering his voice. "But there's a dead body out there. And it's my job to figure out if it was a murder or not."

She nodded slowly as the color drained from her face. "Oh, I see."

"So, you think you can help me?"

"Yes. Yes, of course. What is the name of the guest?"

"Declan Wyler."

The concierge typed on the computer and then stopped. She looked at Amos.

"Wyler. That's funny. I just saw him."

"Really?" Amos perked up. "Do you remember what time?"

"Barely an hour ago. He needed a new room key. Looked like he'd had a rough night."

"Rough, how?"

"Was pretty sunburned. He was dirty and was missing both sleeves of his T-shirt. Like they'd been ripped off."

"Have you seen him leave since then?"

"Not long before you guys ... I mean the cops. Before you got here."

"How do you know it was him?"

She smiled slightly. "Because of his dog. Hard to miss that. We don't allow animals here, so—"

"Did he check out?"

She shook her head. "No."

He might have been coming back, Amos thought. But if what Tenoch said was true and Wyler killed Javier, he highly doubted it.

"Would you like me to get someone to bring you to his room?" Dawn asked.

Amos debated going but decided against it. Instead, he said, "I saw a camera out front. Who runs security here?"

His name was Dwayne. He didn't give Amos a last name as they shook hands. Dwayne was a middle-aged Black guy with a lean physique and broad linebacker shoulders.

"You're with homicide?" Dwayne asked as he closed the door to his command center. Eight TV screens formed a grid along the back wall of the small room.

"Yeah, that's right," Amos said.

"You think it is?"

"What's that?"

"A homicide?"

"That's what I'm trying to find out."

"We don't get those here. Suicides either, really. Only one since I've been on the job."

Amos pointed at the screens. "Got any cameras in the corridor where we found him?"

"I already checked. Can see him coming down, but not where he jumped from." Dwayne sat at the desk with the controls to the TV screens. He tapped and clicked, queuing up the footage on the bottom center screen. Amos watched the footage rolling. Five seconds in, there was a blur as the body came down. A documentary crew would cream their skinny jeans to get their hands on footage like that, he thought.

"Notice anything off in that?" Dwayne asked.

Amos grinned. Dwayne was sharp. Must have been a cop before he was forced into mandatory retirement, Amos guessed.

"What'd you see, Dwayne?" Amos said.

Dwayne rewound the footage and played it at half speed. "Not much movement on the guy. Someone jumps, it's only natural to get some arm or leg movement, even if he wants to end it all. I don't see that in this footage."

"So?"

"I don't know. Could mean nothing. Could mean something. That's your job to find out which."

"And what could the 'something' be?"

"Who can say? Maybe he passed out on the way down from fright. Or ..."

"He was dead already?"

Dwayne shrugged.

"It's one theory anyway," Amos said. "Even if it's improbable."

Dwayne nodded. Amos pointed at the screen again. "Can I see the footage from the front entrance? Go back, maybe an hour and a half."

Dwayne clicked around, switching the center screen to the camera Amos wanted.

"Play that on double speed for me," Amos said.

People zipped in and out of the hotel. Then Amos spotted the dog—the dead giveaway.

"Freeze it on this guy right here," Amos said, leaning over Dwayne's shoulder to point out Wyler. Dwayne scrubbed the timeline slowly until he got a clear frame of Wyler. "Mind if I snap a picture?"

"Go ahead," Dwayne said, shifting back so Amos could photograph the screen with his phone.

"Perfect. Thanks. Alright, go normal speed now."

The footage advanced. Amos watched Wyler hand over the valet ticket and then move out of the way. Amos thought that if the guy got the better of Javier, then he was dangerous. This wouldn't be the same as tracking down his run-of-the-mill gang bangers. And the dog ... that was new. A few minutes later, an older SUV pulled into the frame, and Wyler got in.

"Freeze it on the vehicle," Amos said. He took another picture. "What kind of car do you think that is?"

Dwayne rocked his head side to side in thought. "I don't know. Chevy Blazer, maybe. Could be a Ford Bronco."

"Alright. And how good is your zoom on that camera?"

Dwayne smirked. "The best money can buy."

Without asking, Dwayne advanced the footage and stopped it once the vehicle's rear was fully visible. After two clicks, he zoomed in on the license plate. It was pixelated but sharp enough to make out the numbers and letters.

"Dwayne, my friend," Amos said as a huge grin spread across his face. "You deserve a goddamn raise."

Chapter 13

At eight o'clock, Wyler pulled into the lot of a Motel 6 in the city's northeastern section. The location was desolate and in the polar opposite direction from Rafa's house, which made it an ideal spot to hole up for the night. Exhaustion had set in, and the pain from the sunburn was starting to kick into overdrive. The motel wasn't fancy, but Wyler didn't need fancy at that moment. He needed something discrete and functional. Behind the motel was desert, and in front of it were four highway tracts. He parked in the rear, out of sight of the main road.

In the same lot as the motel was a travel center. Wyler bought a burner phone, painkillers, aloe vera lotion, a tub of Vaseline, two gallons of water, two bags of ice, and the fixings to make peanut butter and jelly sandwiches. He paid for the supplies and the hotel with another hundred from his sock money. Inside the room, Wyler threw his bag on the bed and the groceries on the dresser.

A scent of wet carpet and ancient cigarette smoke permeated every square inch of the tired room. It was a downgrade from his previous accommodations, but at least no one was trying to kill him—yet anyway. The air conditioner rattled, struggling to keep pace with the blistering heat of the desert. After throwing the latch on the door, Wyler jammed the single desk chair under the door handle. There was work to be done, but first, he needed to tend to his and Blackjack's injuries.

Wyler turned on the water in the tub. While it filled, he fixed Blackjack a peanut butter sandwich using the knife he'd gotten off Javier. Then, he dumped one of the bags of ice into the tub. He stripped off his clothes and eased into the freezing water. Initially, it took his breath away, but as the ice numbed his skin, he relaxed. Black and blue marks lined his chest and stomach where Tenoch had kicked him and zapped him with the taser. Thinking of the electricity ripping through his body sent a shiver straight down to his toes. He pictured Tenoch's burning eyes. Then he pictured snuffing the fire out of them. His rage had a target, but he needed to control it carefully. If it got away from him, it could lead to mistakes. Or more mistakes, he clarified to himself. He had trusted Soto. Big fucking mistake right there, buddy. The money had tempted him and he overlooked his instincts because of some code of honor to repay a debt and not be like his father. Stupid. But what was done was done. Beating himself up over the past wasn't going to help him with his future.

As Wyler soaked, his thoughts drifted to the Marriott. He wondered what the police had pieced together about Javier. No one pulled him over during his trek to the motel, which he hoped meant the police weren't aware of the vehicle he was driving yet. Whether or not the faked suicide did its job in buying time was yet to be seen. He wondered how many men Rafa had at his disposal and how far they would go to find him. If they did, he assumed they'd be coming like Javier did to end his life. There'd be no capturing involved. No second chance.

After the ice bath, Wyler dried his lower half and slipped on boxers and jeans. He left off his shirt and coated his arms, neck, and face with a thick layer of aloe vera. Then he popped four Tylenol and got to work on Blackjack. He showered the dog off, dried him with the motel hair blower, and then brushed him for twenty minutes. The last thing Wyler did was slather a coating of Vaseline on Blackjack's cracked pads of his paws.

"Get some rest," Wyler said, patting a spot on the bed. Blackjack hopped up, curled into a ball, and was asleep within five minutes. Feeling refreshed, Wyler pried the burner phone out of the plastic packaging. His first call was to Jon Mack—a former CIA spook turned freelancer. They met during their time in Afghanistan. Mack was brilliant at extracting valuable information from out of thin air. He had a vast database of sources and utilized technology at a Silicon Valley entrepreneur level. And during the Florida operation, Mack had bailed Wyler out of a tough spot.

"How's Las Vegas?" Mack answered after the call clicked through his network of security protocols. Knowing Wyler's location was Mack's way of showing off.

"Unfriendlier than I remember it," Wyler said.

"That doesn't sound good."

Wyler filled him in on everything that happened. When he finished, Mack said, "Christ. Did you call Arlo yet?"

"He's on my list."

"So, what can I do for you?"

"I need background on Ortega."

"Anything in particular you're looking for?"

"I need something that will get him out of his house. Something big that would make him drop everything to handle it. And preferably soon."

"How soon?"

"Tomorrow. A day after that, the latest."

"Oh, so nothing major," Mack said sarcastically.

The sounds of furious typing came through the phone as Mack did his thing.

"Something big, huh," Mack mumbled. "Let's see. Rafa Antonio Ortega. Here he is. He grew up in LA. Raised by a single mother. Did well in school. Graduated from college with a management degree and an engineering minor. Finished top of his class. Got into real estate in Los Angeles after he graduated. Blah, blah, blah. Boring. Nothing useful there."

More typing and clicking.

"Wait a minute," Mack said. "What's this?"

"What do you got?"

"A file from the DEA."

"He was under investigation by the DEA?"

There was a pause, and then Mack said, "No. It's about his father."

"Okay?"

"Hmmm."

"What?"

"Apparently, his father was the head of a drug cartel in Tijuana. Armando Cortes."

"Why the different last name?"

"Who knows. Maybe the mother didn't want her son tied to a drug lord."

"Makes sense."

"Says Cortes was killed in a car bombing by a rival cartel. Rafa was ... twenty at the time."

Wyler grabbed the loaf of bread and fixed himself a sandwich while he talked.

"Okay, what else?" Wyler said.

"And Cortes has a brother, Bruno, who's currently doing a twenty-year stint in San Quentin."

"What's he in for?"

"Let's see ... says he was an accountant and got sentenced for laundering money, among other financial crimes."

Wyler took a bite of the sandwich, thinking. After he swallowed, he said, "Can you see the visitor's log at San Quentin for the uncle?"

"Why do you insult me with questions like that?"

Wyler grinned. "Sorry. Won't let it happen again."

Mack typed and clicked, mumbling his actions as he did. "Access this database ... go through this firewall ... break that code ... and here we go. Visitor logs for Cortes, Bruno."

"Start with this year. Is Ortega on there?"

Mack hummed while he scrolled. Then he said, "Yeah. He's on here. Looks like he visits at least once a month." A few more clicks. "The guy seems pretty consistent as I'm going back through the years."

"That could be something."

"It could be."

"How hard would it be for you to fake a call from the prison?"

Mack sighed. "Again, with the insulting questions."

"Okay. If a call came in ... something urgent about his uncle ... that required him to go out there right away ..."

"I see where you're going," Mack said, then paused. "Playing devil's advocate. Your plan could work, but if Ortega doesn't care about his uncle as much as you think, he might not go for another two weeks. Or maybe he sends someone else."

It was a valid point, but Wyler had to try something. He didn't have the time or the means to do a thorough surveillance to learn Rafa's habits.

"That's the best I've got right now," Wyler said.

"Alright. I can make it happen ... for a price, of course."

Wyler knew that was coming. "How much?"

"Five grand."

Wyler had come to Vegas hoping to rake in close to a quarter of a million dollars. Not only did he not get that, but now he was about to go in the hole. To not have those dogs die a horrible death, though, was worth it.

Without hesitating, Wyler said, "Do it."

Amos turned right off the Vegas strip. He drove for two minutes before pulling into the lot of a 7-11 and a pool hall. It was a far cry from the extravagance of the flashy hotels and casinos a few blocks away. Amos got out and strolled into the pool hall. The place was lit only by the lights above the tables, creating a cave-like atmosphere. It had a gritty charm that Amos found appealing. An old timer with a gray mustache and weathered skin from too much sun and too many cigarettes sat on a stool behind the counter near the entrance. He looked up from scribbling in a Sudoku book, squinting at the newcomer. The old timer recognized Amos and nodded toward the back of the expansive space.

Three of the twelve tables were occupied with people lazily potting balls. Amos meandered through the rows of green felt to the back corner. Harlan Dyson—Dice for short—was hunched over the table, lining up a shot. The nickname was a little on the nose for Amos's tastes, but he never mentioned it. Dice was a transplant from Kentucky. He relocated to Vegas after the Feds closed in on him for 'allegedly' trafficking heroin. Allegedly was the term Dice liked to tack on whenever the subject came up. He wore jeans with cowboy boots and a black t-shirt beneath a checkered flannel shirt with the sleeves cut off, creating a redneck vest. His hair was dirty blonde and three inches shy of forming a mullet. From appearances alone, Dice was hard to take seriously, but beneath the veneer was a shrewd underworld businessman.

Sitting on a stool, watching, was Dice's muscle. An ogre of a man that made Andre the Giant look puny. Everyone called him Atlas since he looked like he could hold the world on his shoulders. The reference to a mythological being impressed Amos. Not all criminals were completely uneducated morons.

"Dee-Tek-Tive Amos," Dice drawled as he took his shot. The three-ball rocketed into the corner pocket with a clank. He straightened out and turned to Amos. "Looking for a game?"

"Not tonight," Amos said, leaning against a support beam. "I'm looking for a vehicle, actually. A vintage Ford Bronco, to be exact. Orange with Jersey plates."

"That's specific," Dice said, pacing around the table, chalking his cue while he decided on his next shot. "As you can see, though, I own a pool hall, not a car dealership."

"This is an easy one for you. I just need eyes on the streets. It's a little time-sensitive, though."

"Is that right?" Dice took a shot, sinking the four-ball, then stood and chalked his cue again. "Why's it so important?"

"Part of an investigation."

"Homicide?"

"I'm a homicide detective, aren't I? Something you think you can handle?"

Dice shrugged. "Last time I checked, you already used up all your credit. This is a clean slate, as they say. So, I'm going to need a little ... incentive."

Amos smiled. He took out his comb, ran it through his hair, then tucked it back in his pocket.

"Okay, how's this for an incentive?" Amos said. "You'd be owed a favor from some ... people of influence."

"Yeah? What people?"

Amos glanced around the hall. No one was within earshot.

He said, "Tenoch Parrada. Rafa Ortega."

Dice stopped chalking his cue and stared at Amos through the hazy light. Then he glanced at Atlas, who raised an eyebrow at the significance of the names.

"You know who they are, I take it?" Amos said.

"I've heard a thing or two," Dice said, resuming his chalking.

"Is that a payment you find to your liking?"

"We just got to find the car? Nothing else?"

"I just need a location. That's it. I can take it from there."

Dice looked at Atlas one more time, then at Amos. "Alright, we got a deal. No promises, though, that I find it. And if I don't, I still am owed for the work done."

"That's fair." Amos pushed off from the support beam. "This is a high-priority job. Remember that. The better you do, the better your reward."

"Yeah, yeah," Dice said, lining up his next shot.

"You got my number. Call me as soon as you have something." Amos stopped and spun on his heels, putting his fingers to his temple like he'd just remembered something. "Oh, and another thing. Have one of your guys call the cops and report a crime. Something violent. Armed robbery or assault. Tell them to give the same description of the vehicle I gave you. Whatever crime you pick, have them say it was a white guy with a dog who committed the offense."

"A dog?"

"Yeah. Say it was something that looked like a German Shepard."

"Okay. Why?"

"That way I can get a BOLO going too." Amos grinned. "Let's see who can find him first."

"Alright, mister copper man, I'll get someone on it."

"Much obliged."

Amos threw a light-hearted salute to the guy behind the register as he left. Outside, Amos climbed into the Charger, pleased with himself. Having Dice on board, combined with an eventual BOLO, increased his chances of catching the elusive man and his dog. Dice was a shady character, but he understood what it meant to be owed a favor by people like Tenoch and Rafa. His people would cover the areas the cops normally wouldn't. Now, all Amos needed to do was wait.

Wyler sat at the small desk by the window with his phone and Javier's gun. He dialed a number, put the phone on speaker, and then began to field strip the weapon. On the fourth ring, a woman answered.

"Who's this?"

"Hey, Mya. It's me, Declan."

"Wyler? What number is this?" Mya Tallulah said.

Like many of Wyler's friends, he met Mya through the military. She was a fellow Marine and mechanical genius who could repair any vehicle, and in the desert loaded with IEDs, her skills were invaluable. Motor oil ran through her veins, and she was as tough as the diesel engines she fixed. After leaving the service, she worked for Ford for several years before opening her own custom shop in San Bernardino. She was the one who restored Wyler's Bronco.

"It's a burner," Wyler said.

"Ah," Mya said. "So this isn't a social call."

"No, unfortunately."

"What's going on?"

Similar to Mack, Wyler walked her through everything that had happened. Then, he outlined his plan. Mya went quiet.

"You still there?" Wyler asked.

"Yup. Just digesting," she said. "You realize that it sounds like you've lost your damn mind, yeah? You should be thanking the heavens you're alive and getting the hell out of there while you still can."

"You know I can't do that."

"I do. And I know if anyone is insane enough to pull off your equally insane plan, it's you."

"Is that your way of saying yes?"

She laughed. "I mean, shit, Wyler, you had me on board as soon as you brought up dogs being involved. Which is messed up if you think about it. Preying on my weaknesses like that."

Wyler grinned as he began to reassemble the gun. "I owe you."

"You bet your scrawny white ass, you do," Mya said. "And I've just got to state the obvious."

"Okay."

Her voice lowered, the laughter gone. "You know this is all

highly illegal?"

"Yes."

"And if we get arrested, you're paying for my lawyer."

"Yes."

"And if we ... get killed ... then I guess I'm just going to have to haunt your ass for all eternity in hell."

"I would expect nothing less. At least I'd have company."

"God damn it, Wyler," Mya said. Then she laughed again, breaking the tension. "Trouble sure has a way of finding you."

Wyler sighed. "It's the cross I have to bear."

"You got a list of the things you need?"

Wyler rattled off some gear he thought would serve them well for the assault on the bunker. Then, he detailed the specs and supplies for getting the dogs out.

"That's quite the list," Mya said.

"Doable?"

"Depends when you need this to happen."

"I've got a play in motion. Whether or not it pans out, I'm waiting to see. How much time would you need for everything?"

"The vehicle won't be a problem. I've already got something I can use with a few tweaks. And the rest of it ..." she paused. "Maybe four or five hours. Then it's about a three-and-a-half-hour drive to Vegas."

Wyler added up the times. Ten hours conservatively. If Rafa took the bait, it could work.

"Alright. Let's do it, then," Wyler said. "I'll hit you up when I get the green light. Appreciate you being flexible...I know I'm asking a lot."

"Yeah, well, just as long as you recognize."

Wyler smiled, "Talk soon." Then he hung up.

Having Mya on board was a huge asset. It evened out the odds stacked against him. Wyler dropped a round into the chamber of the gun. He fed the remaining fourteen rounds into the magazine, then inserted it back into the Hellcat. Things were moving. Being on the offensive for a change felt good. Wyler looked at Blackjack on the bed, sound asleep. Speaking of debts, he owed his life to that dog. How would he ever repay that? Watching Blackjack made Wyler realize how exhausted he was, too. If he was going to pull off his plan, he needed to get rest while he had the chance. He stood, but before getting into the bed, he placed one more call. This one was to Ellie. He just wanted to hear her voice. As the phone rang, he paced the room. She didn't answer. He guessed she didn't pick up because of the unrecognized number or she was working. When it went to voicemail, he said, "Hey, it's me. Lost my phone. Just wanted to check in. I'll call you again tomorrow. Love you."

He froze immediately after saying the words and ending the call. *Love you?* Neither of them had said the words yet. And now he'd just done it through a voicemail. Stupid. Cheesy. He must have been more tired than he thought. But the more he analyzed it, the more he realized he meant it. He did love Ellie. Facing death twice in a twenty-four-hour span apparently did funny things to a man. It brought into focus what was important. Wyler decided at that moment that if he made it home, he'd tell Ellie everything there was to know about him. Even the ugly parts. No more holding back. No more secrets. The words were out there now, and he needed to know, one way or another, if she loved him too.

Chapter 14

After leaving Dice at the pool hall, Amos returned to the JW Marriott. Cameron, Hobart, and Javier's corpse were long gone. The regular hustle and bustle of tourists and hotel activities had returned to normal despite the earlier dark cloud that shrouded the premises. A new concierge was behind the front desk but was equally obliging to allow Amos access to Wyler's room. Amos slipped on a pair of latex gloves before entering. He didn't expect to find anything useful but didn't want to leave any stones unturned. If Wyler was arrested by someone not connected to Rafa, Amos would need evidence to pin Javier's murder on him. And the more damning evidence he had, the easier it would be to discredit any implicating story Wyler told. But the room turned up nothing of value. No apparent signs of a struggle or blood stains.

He went to the balcony and looked over the railing. The crime scene tape blocked off the area where Javier had landed. Amos gauged the trajectory. It was certainly plausible that Javier came from Wyler's room. Proving that was a different story, though. He'd have to wait for the autopsy to come back to show there was foul play involved to push the murder narrative and get CSI in there to sweep the room for evidence.

After leaving the hotel, Amos cruised the streets for a while. He tried to put himself in Wyler's shoes to get a sense of where he might have gone. The airport would be most people's first stop, but based on the vehicle he saw at the hotel with Jersey plates, suggested Wyler drove cross country. Would he try to drive back home? Seemed that was the likely choice. If the guy had any sense at least. If that was the case, then catching him wouldn't be easy. Too many routes out of the city. Amos considered who he could reach out to in Jersey for information. No one came to mind and he dreaded having to go out there. He hated the east coast. Winter and snow didn't agree with him. No. If he or Dice didn't find Wyler within the next twenty-four hours, he'd mark the man as no longer his problem. If Wyler had killed Javier, he wouldn't be eager to talk to the cops despite Tenoch trying to kill him. It'd be a wash. But if for some reason beyond Amos's understanding, Wyler stayed in Vegas, then he had a shot of putting him down.

At midnight, with no leads, Amos returned to the precinct. He spent an hour doing paperwork for other cases. It helped keep him distracted while he waited for any word from the streets. Once he finished that, he went into the 'barracks'—a small section off of the break room that had two couches. It was a spot reserved for cops pulling all-nighters or those with nowhere to go after a fight with their significant other. Amos was too wired to go home. He knew sleep wouldn't find him there either, but he understood the importance of rest. So, he removed his blazer and draped it over the arm of the lesser of the two worn-out couches before lying down.

As Amos stared at the ceiling, he visualized his future. Project what you want into the world, and it'll be yours. That was the new-age drivel advertised by talk shows, anyway. He envisioned surprising Wyler, drawing his gun, and putting two rounds in the man's chest. Then, he'd arrange the facts and evidence to show Wyler was the man wanted in connection with the call put in by Dice's man. At which point, Amos would be called a hero for taking a criminal off the streets. That would solve one problem for Rafa and Tenoch. They'd find a new way to win their land deal, and Amos would make chief. He'd ride that out for two or three years before announcing his run for Congress. Chief Amos. Senator Amos. He smiled at the thought. Maybe the whole projection thing wasn't so stupid after all.

A steady buzz woke Wyler from a deep slumber. He found the phone on the nightstand and answered it.

"Ellie?" he said, still half in a dream.

"Sorry to disappoint, sweetheart," Mack said.

Wyler sat up in bed, rubbing the sleep out of his eyes. "What time is it?"

"Where you are, it's two in the morning." When Wyler didn't respond, Mack said, "You got the green light. Your plan is a go."

"Really?"

"Ortega took the call at ten thirty. I used this new AI tool that emulates a person's voice after hearing them talk for less than thirty seconds. I found a recorded press conference the warden gave at San Quentin last year. The tool worked like a charm.

Ortega had no idea he wasn't talking to the real warden."

"What did you tell him?"

"That something happened with his uncle. I kept things vague, telling him it was better to talk in person as soon as possible. He seemed genuinely concerned."

"So you think he's going to go?"

"I wouldn't be calling you with a hunch. Come on." Mack snorted. "I did some digging and found the airport where Ortega charters a private jet. Then, I hacked into their scheduling system and waited. Ortega was on the books half an hour after the call. Looks like the uncle was a good angle.

"I got lucky."

"Yeah, okay, Mr. Modest.

"When's the flight?"

"In eight hours. Ten a.m."

"What's the total travel time?"

Typing and a few clicks later, Mack said, "Hour and a half in the air, then ... about a fifteen-minute car ride from San Rafael airport. Figure maybe another fifteen minutes to get cleared into the prison. Then another ten or fifteen minutes for him to figure out the story was bullshit."

That would give Wyler two hours to get in and out of the bunker with the dogs. Four hours if Rafa didn't notify anyone back in Vegas once he found out his uncle was okay. Wyler wasn't positive that Rafa would connect him to the misdirection, but to play it safe, Wyler would base his decision on a two-hour clock. The timing would be tight. His and Mya's execution would have to be flawless.

"I appreciate you doing this," Wyler said.

"Don't mention it. My bank account thanks you," Mack said.

"And Wyler ... there's something else."

Wyler held his breath, not liking the sound of Mack's voice. "What's that?"

"There's a BOLO out for you. You're wanted for aggravated assault and battery and to be considered armed and dangerous."

Wyler exhaled slowly, processing the news. Assault and battery? Not murder? So this had to be something other than Javier, at least not directly anyway, Wyler thought. There was no way the police could have ruled the death a homicide that quickly. Where did the charge come from then? Someone on Rafa's payroll within a police department? It seemed the most likely scenario. He shook it off. The information didn't change his resolve or plans. It just meant he had to be more careful driving to his intended rendezvous point with Mya.

"Did you hear me?" Mack said.

"Yeah. Thanks for the heads up."

"Make sure you watch your six, huh?"

"I always knew you cared."

"Don't go spreading rumors now. It's purely a financial comment. With the amount of shit you get into, it'd be a real hit to my bottom line."

Wyler laughed. "Well, thanks for not sugarcoating it."

"Never," Mack said. "Good luck, Wyler."

The call ended. He sat there in the dark, thinking. Having the cops on to him wasn't great, but Rafa taking the bait gave him an opportunity he couldn't pass up, no matter the risks. Getting out of an assault charge was a different story. He pushed the thought aside. That was a concern for another day.

Wyler called Mya. She answered on the sixth ring.

"What's the word?" she asked.

"We're on. We need to hit the target at ten. I'd need you here by nine. Is that possible?"

Silence. Then she said, "I can make it."

"Were you able to get everything?"

"Yeah. I'm just putting the finishing touches on our ride. Where am I meeting you?"

Wyler pulled the phone from his ear and typed an address. "I just texted you the location. Did it come through?"

"I got it."

He then told her about the BOLO. It wouldn't be right to withhold the information from her. If she was involved, she needed to know everything and all the risks that came with it.

"It's not ideal. I know none of it really is," Wyler said. "If you want to back out, though, now's your chance. I wouldn't blame you. And there'd be no hard feelings on my end."

"What, you're trying to shake me loose already?"

"No ... it's just ..."

"I said I was in. That means I'm in. Even if this is batshit crazy. End of story. You've never been one to second guess yourself. Don't start now."

She was right again. When they were overseas, second-guessing and hesitation were what got people killed. And the situation that faced them was no less dangerous.

"I'll see you soon then," Wyler said.

"Count on it." Then she hung up.

Wyler set the phone down. He breathed slowly, settling back into the bed to get a few more hours of rest for the long day ahead.

Amos's phone alarm sounded at six. He turned it off and sat up. His mouth tasted stale, and his deodorant had long since given out. From the bottom drawer of his desk, Amos grabbed a fresh shirt and grooming kit. In the bathroom, he removed his shirt, washed his face, gargled some mouthwash, applied a fresh layer of deodorant, and then slipped on his clean button down. He knotted his tie, then combed his hair. At his desk, Amos checked the computer for any hits on the BOLO for Wyler. There were two logged of a similar vehicle make, but the plates didn't match. He wasn't too surprised. The daily grinders on the force had bigger concerns than looking for one vehicle out of thousands. That left Amos his second source.

Amos scanned the precinct floor. There was more activity now than when he came in earlier, but no one paid him any attention. He took out his second phone and called Dice.

"Morning," Dice said. "I was just thinking about you."

"You got something?"

"My people have been hitting the streets hard. I talk, they listen, you know."

"Get to it."

"Wow," Dice said with feigned hurt. "Here I am busting my balls for you, and I can't get a little bedside manner."

Amos wasn't in the mood for the song and dance. "Do you have anything or not?"

"You must be a real hit with the ladies," Dice said. He sighed, dragging things out. Amos knew the fucker was enjoying himself. "You'll be happy to hear I got five potentials for you."

"That's what you want me to be excited about? Five potentials? No one could confirm the plates?"

"Some of these guys I work with can be a little skittish. They've had the cops called on them one too many times for doing nothing. They start lurking around strangers' cars ... you do the math."

Great, Amos thought. That meant he was dealing with information more than likely from crackheads or the homeless. He massaged his eyebrows, feeling a headache coming on.

"How recent are these sightings?" Amos asked.

"Fresh. Piping hot. Right off the presses."

"But no plate numbers?"

Dice grunted. "Do you want the locations or not? You said you'd handle things from there. You wanted sightings. Well, that's what I've got."

Since Amos had nothing else to go on, he said, "Alright, let's hear them."

Dice listed five addresses, and Amos jotted them down on a small pad.

"So, you're going to put in a word now with your friends?" Dice said.

"Only if one of these addresses pans out."

"That's how you're going to do me? That's not what we agreed to—"

Amos hung up. He tore off the paper with the addresses, grabbed his keys, and went out the precinct door.

The first address Amos drove to was the one closest to the station. He found the vehicle in a lot behind a casino on the strip. It was orange, but that was the only matching detail. For starters, it was a Dodge Challenger, so it was a sedan instead of an SUV. It was modern, and it had Nevada plates. Fucking Dice, Amos cursed to himself. If every vehicle on the list was this blatantly bogus, Amos considered how he could drum up a search warrant and raid the pool hall with two SWAT teams. He would personally enjoy shoving a pool cue up Dice's ass.

The second vehicle turned out a little better. It was at least an older SUV, but it was red, the wrong make, and had New Mexico plates. For the third vehicle, he drove south. His pulse quickened when he pulled into an apartment complex and spotted a vintage Ford Bronco. The color, make, and rough year matched, but the Nevada plates didn't. Those could be stolen and swapped, though, Amos rationalized. He parked and ran the plate numbers. They came back, matching the address of where Amos was. That ruled another one out. He slapped the steering wheel until his hand stung. After the anger subsided, Amos collected himself and headed for the next address, which was another bust.

Annoyed, he stopped at a coffee shop for breakfast. He ordered a bagel with cream cheese and a black coffee. The order came out five minutes later. Amos set the coffee on the cruiser's hood, electing to eat outside instead of inside the car. He hated it when his colleagues did that. It left the car a mess and him smelling like a diner. *Slobs. He worked with classless slobs.* It was eight thirty, so the heat was manageable at that point, but the city would be baking soon. He'd been searching for Wyler for close to two and a half hours already and was beginning to think finding the man wouldn't happen. As Amos ate his bagel, he studied the list of addresses. One to go. He put the location into his phone. It popped up as being at a Motel 6 in the northeastern part of the city. On the outskirts, he thought. Sipping on his coffee, he debated bailing and going to the pool hall to harass Dice for the shit intel. But then he thought about Tenoch and Rafa. For people like them, he needed to do his due diligence. That way, if he delivered bad news, it was at least backed by thoroughness.

Amos pounded the rest of his coffee, crumpled the wrapper, and tossed the trash. Before getting in, he combed his hair, using the window as a mirror. Then he climbed in and fired the ignition. Traffic picked up as the work day kicked off. Amos cursed and honked until he made it through the worst of it. The Motel 6 was sandwiched between a service station and a loading depot. Big rig trucks littered the landscape.

"Waste of time," Amos grumbled as he eased past the motel's entrance. The cars in the lot were mostly beaters. Nothing remotely resembling what he was looking for. He was about to call it quits when something caught his attention to the right as he passed the edge of the hotel. A hundred yards away, reversed into a parking spot, was a late model, orange SUV. But that wasn't what caused his heart rate to spike. Walking across the pavement was a man with a dog at his side. Amos was too far away to make a positive ID from the Marriott security footage, but the signs all pointed to this being his man.

Amos quickly cut the wheel and reversed into a parking spot. He considered his options for how to handle the situation. Wyler and the dog got into the Bronco already. Amos could gun it and try to block the vehicle from leaving, get out, and unload his gun into the windshield. A shock and awe approach, but that was too flashy. The distance was too far. If the guy was former military and was already spooked, seeing a speeding, unmarked car flying at him would only make him react violently. Plus, it was just open desert behind him. No way to entirely block off an escape. Amos considered approaching slowly. Come in non-threatening to get the man to pause, then blow his head off. But that left Amos exposed and presented far too many risks for his own personal safety.

The only option that left Amos was to tail the Bronco. Play the patient game and wait for a better chance to strike. Amos didn't want to involve the force if he didn't have to. The fewer witnesses to Wyler's demise, the better. But in the worst-case scenario, Amos knew he could call in backup to assist in stopping Wyler from fleeing. If it came to a standoff, that played into Amos's favor for using deadly force. He kept the car in drive with his foot on the brake while he slipped his gun out of the holster. He pulled the slide back a half inch, ensuring a round was in the chamber. Satisfied, Amos tucked the gun into the cup holder for easy access. Then, he waited for Wyler to make the first move.

Chapter 15

Wyler clipped Blackjack into his safety harness. Then, his fingers coiled around the grip of the Hellcat. The unmarked cruiser hadn't moved yet. At first, he thought it was just a coincidence. But when the cruiser stopped and backed into the spot, Wyler thought otherwise. How could the police have found him already? Sweat began forming on his neck, and not from the sunburn. How many other cops were there? Was he in a net already and didn't know it? Was he about to be caught or worse, riddled with bullets? He tamped down the fears, his eyes glued to the black Charger. Whoever it was, they weren't moving. Why? Did they want him to drive off first? Or had he completely misjudged their interest in him?

On the center console screen, Wyler input the casino address where he planned to meet with Mya. It was only ten miles away. Less than a fifteen-minute drive. But if cops were going to be tailing him, he needed an unconventional route to get there. Wyler pinched and zoomed on the screen, searching for an idea. He glanced up at the Charger. The Charger was a rear-wheel drive car, from what he remembered. In an open straightaway, the Bronco's engine was no match for the hefty V8 engine of the Charger. He wouldn't be able to outrun it—on pavement, anyway. Wyler smiled at the prospect. He turned to Blackjack.

"Hold on, boy. It's going to be a rough ride."

Blackjack barked once. Wyler tucked the gun into his pants, then shifted into drive. His heartbeat matched the rhythm of the engine's pistons. He drove out of the parking spot following the path that looped behind the motel. His eyes danced back and forth between the rearview mirror and the road ahead of him. The horizon looked clear. No signs of other cop cars. Wyler stopped at the exit to the lot. Turning right led him to the highway. Left toward the desert. He waited a second, watching the rearview. The Charger appeared fifty yards back. Wyler turned left and kept his speed around thirty. If the Charger followed him, he knew it was on. If it didn't, he figured he had just been paranoid and didn't need to worry. Wyler saw the Charger approach the exit to the lot. It stopped. Wyler held his breath, willing the car to turn right. When it didn't, he exhaled slowly. The decision was made. If the cops wanted him, they would have to catch him first.

Thirty yards ahead, the road split left and right at ninety degrees. Beyond that point, if roads existed, they were dirt only, precisely what Wyler wanted. At the intersection, Wyler glanced both ways. No cars coming in either direction. He took one last look in the rearview. The Charger was keeping its distance but definitely was following him.

"Here we go," Wyler said. His knuckles turned a shade of white as he gripped the steering wheel. Then he pressed the gas pedal to the floor. The Bronco jumped off the line. The electric engine hurled them forward like an Olympic sprinter. He crossed the intersection and thumped onto the desert floor. The tires bit into the dirt and quickly gained traction. Wyler stayed on a straight line going north. The GPS showed a stretch of train track cutting through the desert. He wanted to make the ride on the Charger as rough as possible. Going over steel tracks at speed was sure to wreak havoc with the lower suspension of the Dodge.

The speedometer crept into the seventies. Wyler glanced in the rearview again. The Charger was following him but had already lost ground. Two minutes later, Wyler saw the train tracks. He raced towards them. At the last possible second, he braked hard, slowing the Bronco to five miles an hour. The SUV bumped up and over the tracks with ease. Once all four wheels were on dry earth again, Wyler punched the throttle. He kept the Bronco headed north, wanting to draw the cop away from civilization and reinforcements. A mountain range loomed three hundred yards ahead. A glance in the rearview showed the Charger hitting the tracks. Sparks flew out from underneath the car as it went over. Wyler grinned.

Stop smiling, he told himself. You're not out of this yet.

Wyler drove on, angling the Bronco between two outcroppings of a craggy mountain. It took him a minute to find the dirt road on the GPS. The two-wheel rut path snaked its way through the rugged terrain as if centuries ago, it had been a flourishing river. A mile later, as the mountains closed in on Wyler, he lost sight of the Charger. Whoever was chasing him either gave up or had lost a lot of ground. Wyler kept his senses on high alert. The possibility existed for the cop, if it was indeed a cop, to call in air support. If a helicopter got involved, Wyler was screwed. In the open landscape, he'd be exposed for miles. He kept his speed up as the trail gradually curved west. Twenty minutes later, the land flattened out again.

The trail spit Wyler out about fifteen miles north and slightly to the west of his target. As the Bronco angled south, Wyler held his breath again, scanning the horizon for the black dot of the car. If the Charger was still searching, Wyler couldn't see it. He rolled down the window, letting in the warm air, and listened for the dull beat of a helicopter. It was a sound he knew well but one that he thankfully didn't hear. The hot breeze coursed over his tender skin like an army of fire ants. He left the window open. The pain kept his senses firing on all cylinders. Blackjack groaned, spreading his legs to remain upright as the Bronco bound over an unseen crater in the ground.

"Sorry," Wyler said. "We're almost out of this."

Wyler stuck as close to the mountains as possible on the offhand chance his pursuer guessed the looping route he took. He cut the wheel, turning east. In the distance, he saw a patch in the landscape indicating a man-made structure.

Then he heard gunfire.

His muscles tensed, and Wyler instinctively slouched in the seat. He looked around frantically for the source of the shooting. As he barrelled forward, the sound increased. Nothing hit the Bronco, though. No broken glass. No slugs slamming into the sheet metal. Then there was more gunfire, but the pitch sounded like different calibers. It didn't make sense. He checked the GPS to see what the structure ahead of him was. When he read the words, his muscles relaxed. A shooting range. Wyler sat up straighter behind the wheel and shook his head, feeling foolish. His nerves were more frayed than he thought. The momentary scare sobered Wyler to the stakes involved with what he was doing. Misplay a move, and it could cost him and Blackjack their lives.

The final stretch of desert lay in front of him. Wyler cut the wheel to the right, heading south. He steered wide of the shooting range and pushed the speed. The Bronco kicked up a cloud of dust. Civilization came into focus. A suburban sprawl appeared. The GPS showed he was only five miles away from the casino. Reaching the rows of houses would provide him a degree of coverage. His grip relaxed on the steering wheel. He was almost there. With his attention focused on the peaks of the sun-bleached homes, Wyler almost missed the roadblock in front of him. He just caught the glint of sun on metal, forcing him to brake and spin the wheel to avoid slamming into a wire rope fence.

Wyler wiped a new bead of sweat from his forehead, and then got out of the Bronco. He walked to the blockade. Thigh-high wooden posts supported two thick cables. They were spaced at fifteen-foot intervals. Wyler shielded his eyes as he looked left and then right. The blockade stretched as far as he could see. Not good. He checked his watch. It was 9:45 AM. The detour put him behind schedule. Rafa's flight was at 10 AM, leaving Wyler a two-hour window to get the dogs out safely. He needed every minute to get that done. And for all he knew, the blockade surrounded a broad section of the city. Driving until he found an opening could set him back even further. To retain any time advantage, he needed to enter here.

Wyler gripped the wire and pulled, testing the strength of the hold. The wire didn't budge. He considered getting the Bronco up to speed and trying to ram through it, but that risked severe damage to the vehicle without guaranteeing success. His other option was to leave the Bronco and cover the rest of the distance on foot. That brought its challenges, and he dismissed it for the time it would waste. Wyler opened the back door of the Bronco and lifted the floor, searching the storage compartment for anything useful. There was a Crovel—a military-grade multitool shovel—that he could try to pry loose the wire or dig out a pole. But again, that would take too much time. He put the Crovel back and rummaged through more of his gear, stopping when he picked up his camping stove. He glanced back at the wires and where they connected to the wood pole. An idea formed. It could work.

Sweat soaked Wyler's shirt as he dug out a roll of duct tape and removed the two palm-sized fuel canisters from the camping stove. He hustled to the blockade, where he taped one canister at the top intersecting point of the wire to the pole and one at the bottom. Then he hopped in the Bronco and drove to a safer distance, twenty feet away. He unclipped Blackjack.

"In the back," Wyler said.

Blackjack did as he was told, and then Wyler took his spot in the passenger seat. After rolling the window down, he pulled out the handgun. The clock ticked away in his head. He wiped the perspiration from his hands on his pants. This is going to work, he told himself, screwing the suppressor back onto the barrel. He waited until no cars were coming on the street inside the blockade. Then he steadied his breathing, aimed the gun, kept both eyes open, and squeezed the trigger. The suppressor did its job muffling the sound of the shot. The bullet struck the top canister. A dull pop was followed by a sharp crack of splintering wood as the aluminum canister exploded. Wyler dropped the barrel a few inches and fired again. Another pop. He put the gun away and squinted at the posts. The wires were still attached, but they drooped substantially.

The timer in Wyler's head kept ticking. He needed to move. The mini explosions weren't the loudest thing in the world, but he didn't want to stick around to see if anyone investigated. After jumping out of the Bronco, he ran to the poles. The wires splayed like frizzy hair and a sizable chunk of wood was dislodged. A few kicks weakened their hold further but they didn't completely give way. They looked loose enough now for the Bronco to do the rest of the work. In theory anyway. It was a gamble now. Either it worked, or it didn't. He was out of options and time. If the Bronco couldn't plow through the crippled defenses, then they would have to go on foot. Wyler returned to the driver's seat, then reclipped Blackjack into his harness.

"Hold on tight," Wyler said as he reversed far enough away to build up speed.

Wyler gripped the steering wheel and locked on to a point of aim where the wire looked the weakest. A picture of Soto and the caged dogs formed in Wyler's mind. This is going to work. For them.

His jaw clamped tight as he hit the gas. The tires dug in and launched the Bronco forward. Thirty miles an hour, then forty. The speedometer kept climbing as the engine hummed. At the moment before impact, Wyler locked his arms and braced for the worst.

Steam poured out of the engine of the Charger as Amos steered it back onto the pavement. The check engine light had come on shortly after he had gone over the train tracks. When the Bronco disappeared into the mountains, Amos decided to cut his losses before he got stranded. He cursed himself for stupidly taking the bait and following Wyler into the desert. The maneuver had caught him off guard. Now, he needed to figure out what to do next. As Amos limped the battered car back to the precinct, he called in a sighting of the Bronco and gave his best guess as to where Wyler had gone.

The attendant at the carpool shook his head at Amos and the Charger like a disappointed parent catching a teen sneaking in past curfew.

"What the heck happened?" the attendant said.

"A perp took me on a bit of a joy ride," Amos said, tossing him the keys.

"You know these cars aren't tanks, right?"

"Yeah, I got that."

"I don't envy you and the sea of paperwork you'll need to fill out."

"Let's just move this along, alright?"

After filling out an initial report, Amos returned to his cubicle inside the station. While he rocked in his chair, stewing, he tried to put himself in Wyler's mind. Why was he still in Vegas? If he were in Wyler's position, he'd be on the first flight to Australia to disappear. So what was keeping him here? Why stay? Why risk getting caught? And Wyler picked up that he was a cop and fled? Why hadn't he reported anything to the police? The only answer was that he didn't trust them. Knew people like himself were connected to Ortega.

Amos headed to the bathroom, where he splashed water on his face and then dried it with a coarse paper towel. He left and went outside and made a call with his secondary phone to Tenoch to cover his ass. The smart move was to inform his partner of what happened and let him know he was trying. When no one answered, Amos hung up. Declan Wyler was turning out to be a more formidable threat than anticipated. Amos stared into the sky and wondered out loud, "Why are you still here?"

Chapter 16

The Bronco rammed into the wire blockade doing close to seventy miles an hour. The connecting bolts tore loose, sending the wires snapping like a whip. Wyler heard a clang of metal on metal. He checked the dashboard for any lights flickering, indicating a problem. None appeared as the Bronco plowed forward.

"There we go," Wyler exhaled with a grin and a glance at Blackjack. "I told you it'd work."

Blackjack ignored him, too busy bracing himself as the SUV skidded onto the paved street. Wyler followed the GPS through the residential neighborhood. He constantly checked his rear-view mirror for flashing lights. Only four miles separated him and the casino. It wasn't far, but plenty of things could still go wrong. Wyler's body remained coiled. Every stop sign, every traffic light, where he wasn't moving, created tension in his gut.

After ten minutes of sweat-inducing driving, he spotted his

destination. A steady stream of elderly people ambled from their cars toward the modern-designed building. Wyler navigated the lot until he reached the parking garage at the rear of the sprawling casino. The wheels squeaked as the Bronco wound its way up the levels. Wyler circled each one until he found who he was looking for.

Mya Tallulah leaned against a customized Ford Econoline van. The vehicle was painted in a hue matching the desert. Massive tires jutted out from the four-wheel wells, giving the van nearly three feet of lift. The suspension looked like it could withstand a fall from the Empire State Building. Three circular lights rode on the front of the grill.

Wyler reversed into the spot next to the van. He unclipped Blackjack, and then they both hopped out. Coming around the front of the Bronco, Wyler took in Mya. She matched his height, just shy of six feet, but her stylish sculpted black hair pulled tight into a near mohawk gave her an extra four inches. Her face was evenly proportioned, with a thin nose and arching eyebrows that gave a fierceness to her look. Mahogany skin matched mahogany eyes. She wore snug jeans and a loose black tank top. Her presence demanded respect. She was pure grit rolled into a beautiful body of class.

"I thought you weren't coming," Mya said, tapping her watch.

"I had to take a bit of a detour," Wyler said. "That's quite the ride."

"For you, only the best."

They hugged. As Mya pushed away, she stared at Wyler.

"Jesus, haven't you ever heard of suntan lotion?"

"I knew I forgot something."

She looked over Wyler's shoulder at the Bronco. "How's she

been running for you?"

"Good. Just got us out of some heavy off-roading."

"I can see that," she said, stepping past him and swiping her finger through a layer of dirt plastered on the hood.

"And what's this tank you brought?" Wyler said, nodding at Mya's ride. "Looks like something the military wouldn't mind having."

"It might be. That's strictly off the record, of course," She grinned. "Figured this was as good an opportunity as I would get testing it under a high-stress scenario. It's got a 7.3L V-8 engine. A Torq Shift 5-speed transmission and a partial military wrap leaf shackle suspension system. It should handle this terrain like it's driving on fresh asphalt." She popped the handle and opened the side doors. The interior was spacious and clean. Climbing inside, she pointed at modern enclosures stacked and bolted against the side and rear walls. "I modified these based on the number of dogs you mentioned. It was a tight squeeze, but they should be more than comfortable. I've got a bunch of other bells and whistles embedded in this bad boy, but I won't bore you with the details."

"And how'd you make out with the rest of the gear?"

"I've got it all."

"Good. Let's double-time it, then. We're already behind schedule."

"Alright." Mya opened the driver-side door of the van, grabbed a screwdriver, and tossed it to Wyler. "For your plates."

Wyler quickly removed the license plates from the Bronco. He stuffed them into his bag before tossing it inside the van. Mya then handed him a corner of a storage tarp. Together, they worked the fabric over his vehicle. The cover wouldn't stop the cops from eventually finding it, but it would at least prevent casino goers from seeing it and reporting a sighting. For Wyler, the garage was as good a place as any to stash the Bronco while he worked.

"Ready?" Mya said.

"Ready."

The three of them piled into the van and set off to rescue some dogs.

Halfway into the drive, Mya said, "Why do you think this guy does it?"

"What guy?" Wyler said.

"Our guy. Ortega. Why would he risk having anything to do with fighting dogs? He's clearly got money. He's got status." Mya glanced at Wyler. "Doesn't make sense to me. You said they wanted you to train their dogs to win a land deal, but it has to go deeper than that. This bunker you described doesn't just happen overnight. Take the land deal out of it. They're still fighting dogs. What's the appeal?"

Wyler shrugged. "Who knows why people do what they do, but I got the sense it was something personal from the past. A bond maybe he shared with his father over dog fights. Learned to turn that caring part of himself off when he was young."

"That's fucked up."

"Or it could just be a thrill for him. He gets off on doing something illegal right under people's noses. Could be boredom. When they get so rich, some guys don't know what to do with themselves. So then they start getting into dark shit."

"That's what they busted that quarterback for, right? What's his name?"

"Vick."

"That's right. Vick. And the Feds just busted someone in the

Department of Defense for doing the same thing."

"Yeah, I heard about that."

"I read the DOD guy could face a max of five years in prison. Can you believe that shit? Five years. Countless dogs killed over a decade and five years is what he faces. And what did Vick do for time?"

"Less than two years, if I remember right," Wyler said. "And he got to play again after."

"Fucked. Up." Mya shook her head. "I just can't wrap my head around how someone has that inside them to do that to a dog. I mean, shit, we're no strangers to death. We enlisted into a program that trained us to dole it out. I'm not trying to be holier than thou. But at least the people we went after could shoot back. These dogs are defenseless."

Wyler nodded. Talking about it stoked the flames of rage inside him.

"That's why if we don't do it, no one will," Wyler said. "That's why I can't walk away. I can't have their deaths hanging on me."

"I get it. I wouldn't be here if I didn't."

The van fell silent, then. Wyler sensed the morality hardening inside Mya against the laws they were about to break. He felt it, too. The words weren't spoken, but Wyler knew Mya was as resolved as he was to see the job through despite the risk posed to their own lives. What she was sacrificing wasn't lost on Wyler. Another personal debt would truly be owed to her far greater than any financial one. It was a debt he was willing to pay ten times over.

They made good time through the city, entering the arid wasteland to the north. Mya stopped the van two miles away from Rafa's house. Wyler opened the back door and then kicked open the legs of a tripod that supported a telescope. He twisted the dials until he was zoomed in on the multi-million dollar home. The time on his phone read 10:20 AM. His jaunt through the mountains to shake the cop cost him twenty precious minutes. They had, at the most, an hour forty left to execute the plan.

"Anything?" Mya asked from the front seat.

Wyler swept the telescope back and forth. "Looks quiet." He leaned back from the eyepiece, then called Mack. When he answered, Wyler asked his question without a hello.

"What's the flight status?"

Okay with no formal greeting, Mack typed away on his keyboard, then said, "It took off on time with your passengers on it. The scheduled arrival time hasn't changed."

"Thanks," Wyler said and hung up. He turned to Mya. "We're a go."

Wyler folded the tripod, closed the door, and got in the passenger seat.

"Head straight towards the house. You'll eventually see a man-made dip in the ground. That's our target."

Mya threw the hulk of a vehicle into drive and hit the gas. The massive tires and suspension made it feel like they were cruising over glass. Neither of them spoke. Wyler felt his heart thumping against his chest. His palms sweat, being back to the location where he was almost killed. A tingling sensation radiated over his burnt skin as if he were under the blazing sun again. He shook the thoughts off and focused on his breathing. For a brief second, he was transported back in time, inside a Humvee approaching a hostile village in Iraq. He wondered if Mya felt the same but he didn't bother asking. At this stage, avoiding unnecessary words was ideal. The fewer distractions, the better.

A hundred yards off, Wyler noticed a subtle dip in the landscape. He pointed.

"You see it?"

Mya nodded. "I've got it." She adjusted the van's course to come in alignment with the gully.

When they got closer, Wyler said, "Okay, slow down. We're looking for another hole." He swallowed away a lump, thinking of what the hole, or rather, grave, contained. An image of Soto's corpse flashed through his mind, stirring up a nauseating wave through Wyler's gut. "It'll be near where the rear hatchway is. That's our point of entry."

"Roger," Mya said.

It took a few passes, but Wyler eventually found the grave. Seeing that it hadn't been filled yet twisted Wyler's stomach a little tighter. He pointed out the hatchway.

"The pry bars are in the compartment in the floor," Mya said as she reversed the van towards the bunker's hidden exit. Wyler climbed in back, grateful to have a task to take his mind off Soto's remains. He spun the latch on the floor and swung open the door. He pulled out two pry bars, a hammer, and a metal wedge from the dark confines. Mya killed the engine and got out. Wyler opened the side door.

"Get me that bag," she said.

Wyler slid over a duffle bag that could easily conceal a body. Mya unzipped a pocket and took out two black bandanas with eye holes cut out of them. She tossed one to Wyler. It had a skull screen printed on it.

"A bit dramatic, isn't it," he said, tying it around his head.

She shrugged. "You said you wanted masks. You didn't specify which kind."

"Fair."

When she finished tying her mask, Wyler handed her one of the pry bars. They hustled to the door.

"Blackjack," Wyler said, motioning with two fingers from his eyes to the house. "Watch."

Blackjack trotted off a few yards to act as an alarm system. His highly tuned senses would catch anyone approaching long before Wyler could. Wyler forced the metal wedge into the thin gap between the hatchway door and the frame. Then, he used the hammer to drive the wedge deeper. From the space created, Wyler and Mya inserted their pry bars and pushed. After ten seconds of continued pressure, the lock gave way with a satisfying ping. Mya kept the tension on her bar while Wyler pulled out his gun and aimed it at the hatchway. Using the fingers on his left hand, he counted down from three. When he made a fist, Mya cranked on the pry bar, raising the door far enough for Wyler to see inside. The sliver of light showed the stairwell was empty.

"Clear," Wyler said, pushing the hatchway fully open. "Let's get the rest of the gear."

They hustled back to the van. Wyler tossed the bars back into the storage area while Mya opened the main section of the duffle bag. She pulled out two crossbows. They were black with a stock similar to an assault rifle. Unlike a traditional crossbow, the tension arms were tucked close to the frame.

"What the hell are these?" Wyler asked.

"Some new compact crossbows," she said, cocking the wire back and loading in a bolt.

Wyler raised an eyebrow. "That's ... an interesting choice."

"Listen, we needed weapons, preferably quiet ones that didn't require a permit to purchase. I paid cash for these, which leaves no trace to us. If we have to ditch them, again, it doesn't tie to us." She elbowed Wyler. "Come on, these are great options for such short notice."

"I can't argue with that." Wyler loaded in a bullet point tipped bolt, then snapped the three extra ones onto the rail beneath the weapon.

Mya tossed him a walkie-talkie next. "Channel three, in case we get separated." After clipping it to her belt, she slung a backpack on. "The rest of the gear is in here. Then we'll come back for the harnesses. Right?"

"Right," Wyler said. Having Mya by his side was reassuring. Her smarts and efficiency added a whole new dynamic to the operation. The three of them created a powerful combat-ready unit that could take on an imposing force. Wyler almost felt bad for anyone who stood in their way. Almost.

"Blackjack will go in first, I'll follow, then you cover the rear."

Mya nodded, closed the doors to the van, and locked it.

Wyler called out to Blackjack. "On me."

When Blackjack arrived at his side, they moved in tandem. At the hatchway, Wyler pointed. "Down."

Blackjack navigated the stairs, stopping at the door leading into the training facility of the bunker. Wyler's breathing quickened and his pulse raced as he arrived at the bottom of the steps. Adrenaline began to surge through his system. He was about to put two of his closest friends directly into harm's way. He held the ramifications of that fact close to his heart. No mistakes, he told himself. Stay sharp. Wyler took a deep breath, then opened the door.

"Search," Wyler whispered to Blackjack.

The dog silently seeped through the slit. Wyler counted in

his head to ten, then flung the door open. He shouldered the crossbow and swept for targets. Mya came in behind him. She turned right while Wyler went straight. Two seconds later, there was a shout, then a growl, then a scream. Wyler spun to his right. A scrawny guy tumbled out from behind a supply self. Blackjack was clamped onto the guy's arm as he rode him to the ground. Wyler and Mya rushed forward. Wyler got there first, grabbing Blackjack by the collar, and shouted, "Release!" Once Blackjack did, Wyler backpedaled out of the way. Mya moved in, leveling her crossbow at the guy's chest.

"On your stomach, now," Mya shouted.

The guy writhed around, moaning and gripping his arm. Mya kicked him in the side and repeated the command. Reluctantly, he rolled over. Mya dropped the backpack.

"You got him?" Mya said to Wyler.

"I got him," Wyler replied, ready to launch the bolt if the guy moved.

Mya pulled zip ties from the pack and quickly bound the guy's wrists. Once he was secured, she rolled him back over and propped him into a seated position.

"What the fuck is this?" the guy said through gritted teeth. He blinked, trying to make sense of what was happening. His eyes were beady and floated high, exposing a sea of white below the iris, giving him a constant dazed appearance.

"How many other people are down here?" Wyler asked.

The guy glanced from Mya to Wyler to Blackjack. His mouth hung open. When he didn't respond, Wyler slapped him across the face.

"Hey. How many other people are down here?"

The slap snapped the guy into focus. "What ... guys ... uh ...

two … two other guys …"

"Are they armed?"

The guy shrugged. "I don't know."

"What do you mean you don't know?" Mya said.

"There's … there are guns around … but … but … we usually just use them for the … for the dogs."

"Fuck him," Mya said, "We should keep moving."

"Let's tie him to the treadmill."

"What do you fuckers want?" the guy said as Wyler and Mya pulled him to his feet.

"Shut up," Wyler said.

"Should we gag him?" Mya asked.

Wyler nodded. After binding the guy to the treadmill, Mya looped three zip ties together. She cut part of the sleeve from the guy's shirt, stuffed it in his mouth, and then tightened the zip tie around his head. Wyler checked the time. 10:30 AM. One room cleared. They needed to pick up the pace.

"Come on," Wyler said. He led the way to the next door that connected to the kennel area. They entered in the same order as the last room. No one was there except for the dogs.

"Jesus," Mya said, stepping inside.

Wyler barely heard her over the sudden onslaught of barking. The familiar smell of piss, shit, and dander was heavy in the air. One pitbull rammed his face into the bars of his cage, frothing from the mouth as Blackjack darted past.

"This is fucked," Mya said.

"Where are the treats?" He felt the rage pounding in his heart, wanting out. But he pushed it back down. Now wasn't the time to unleash it.

"Front pouch."

Wyler moved behind Mya and took out a bag of dog treats laced with Acepromazine. It was a strong sedative that would make the dogs more manageable to handle. Wyler went to each cage, ten total, and shoved a treat through the grates. The dogs wasted no time in scarfing them down.

"Thirty minutes," Wyler said, and the dogs should be out cold. He checked the time on his phone. That would put them at just past eleven o'clock, leaving them roughly an hour to get the dogs out. In the meantime, Wyler knew they needed to secure the rest of the bunker to avoid any surprises. After returning the pouch to the pack, Wyler tapped Mya on the shoulder, and they hustled off toward the next door. The dogs went berserk as they ran by. Wyler shouldered the door open. The hallway was empty. When the door closed behind them, the silence returned. A static hum lingered in Wyler's ears.

"You think the pills are going to work on them?" Mya said. "They were fucking amped."

"They'll work," Wyler said, even though a speck of doubt crept up his spine. If they didn't … then they would just have to make do. Wyler pointed forward. "Up ahead, a hall to the right leads to the main exit. We'll go past that, then there's a lounge on the right. We hit that, then we'll proceed to the arena, which is the last room. Once we clear that, we get the harnesses, then fall back to the kennel."

"Roger that."

Wyler nodded, raised his crossbow, and proceeded up the corridor with Mya close behind. Upon reaching the corner of the next turn, Wyler signaled for Blackjack to move forward. After waiting for five seconds, Wyler advanced, and Blackjack joined them at the intersection leading to the bunker's main entrance.

They found the hallway leading out empty and continued their mission to the lounge without any resistance. Even with the operation going smoothly, Wyler was on edge. He knew from experience that even the best-laid plans could not account for every variable, and the lack of any complications often indicated that something was wrong. The feeling stuck with him as he opened the door to the lounge and sent Blackjack inside. And instead of hearing silence, someone shouted. Wyler knew things were about to get ugly.

Chapter 17

Four men occupied the lounge, double what they were told were still in the bunker. Wyler quickly analyzed the room. Sitting on the couch was Xolo. At the bar, a black guy used a toothpick to extract something from a gold tooth, and directly to the right was the NFL lineman—the same two men Wyler saw in the arena restraining the pit bulls in the ring a day ago. Planted in the chair where Wyler had been tortured was another Hispanic dressed in all black like an undertaker. None of the men immediately moved. It wasn't until Blackjack sprinted towards Xolo that things started to happen.

Xolo tried scrambling up the back of the couch. The memory of Blackjack's bite lined his face. Blackjack latched onto his ankle and dragged him down. He screamed in terror. The undertaker made the first move after that. He shot up and reached for his hip. Wyler aimed and fired the crossbow without waiting to see what he pulled. *Twap*. The bolt rocketed into the groove between the undertaker's shoulder and collarbone, dropping him to his knees. The lineman sprang off the couch with a quick burst of speed. He barrelled into Wyler, taking them both to the ground.

Xolo continued to scream as Mya entered. Gold Tooth recovered from his initial shock and lunged at her with a folding knife. With barely a second to react, Mya raised the crossbow as a shield. The blade entered into the complex web of parts. Mya twisted the weapon, ripping the knife away. Gold Tooth swatted the crossbow from Mya's hands, then sent an elbow towards her face. She dodged the blow and sidestepped while simultaneously pushing Gold Tooth away. The move created separation. The man was outmatched, and in a matter of five seconds, he understood why. Mya fired a devastating kick to Gold Tooth's right knee. As his body instinctively hunched forward, Mya rammed her knee into his nose. The sound of shattering cartilage mixed with Xolo's screams created a horrifying soundtrack. Gold Tooth's body went limp and folded to the floor.

Wyler didn't hear the body drop behind him. He was too focused on the lineman's onslaught. A meaty forearm pressed against Wyler's throat while a sledgehammer fist connected with the side of his sternum. The assault flared Wyler's skin and strained his bruised ribs. A searing heat spread through his chest as oxygen struggled to enter his lungs. Wyler felt like he was drowning. He needed air. The lineman's eyes were lifeless, revealing no opposition to killing him. Another fist landed, sending a sheet of fog over Wyler's vision. Another few seconds and he would pass out. He needed to act quickly. Shuffling his legs, Wyler slipped his left one between the lineman's. He drove his knee up into the man's groin. The lineman howled in pain. His head jerked back, releasing the forearm from Wyler's throat. Then, there was a loud crack of hard plastic against bone. The lineman swayed. As the fog cleared, Wyler saw Mya swing the crossbow. Another loud crack rang out as the butt of the weapon connected with the lineman's head. His body twitched, then pitched to the side. Wyler shuffled out from underneath the unconscious body.

"I had him ..." Wyler coughed. "... the whole time."

"Sure you did," Mya said, helping Wyler to his feet. He took deep breaths, trying to slow his racing heart. The adrenaline surging through him dulled the pain of his inflamed skin and ribs. That could have gone bad in too many ways, Wyler thought. If Mya hadn't agreed to help, he very well might have been killed.

Wyler walked to Blackjack and grabbed him by the collar. "Release."

Once he did, Wyler saw a blood stain seeping into Xolo's pant leg. The terror froze the man to the point of paralysis. He mumbled in Spanish, not bothering to check the wound on his ankle. Mya removed the pistol from the undertaker and shoved him onto the couch.

"Keep an eye on them," Wyler said. "I'll secure these two."

Wyler dragged Gold Tooth to the bar. Keeping him lying down, Wyler zip-tied Gold Tooth's wrists to a support beam of the bar. Getting the lineman next to Gold Tooth proved more challenging. Wyler's muscles strained, dragging the dead weight, but he eventually got there and repeated the binding method.

"You're up," Wyler said to Xolo. When he didn't move, Wyler said, "Blackjack, speak."

Blackjack lunged at him, barking. Xolo put up his hands defensively. "Okay, okay, okay," he shouted. "I'll go." Xolo pushed off the couch and limped to the bar, where Wyler secured him. The undertaker glared at Mya. She responded by cocking the hammer of his gun.

"Try something," Mya said. "I enjoy watching men bleed."

Outnumbered and outgunned, the undertaker joined the others, holding the arrow in his collarbone.

"What should we do about this?" Mya asked, nodding at the arrow.

"Leave it in. Yank it, and he might bleed out."

"And that's a bad thing?"

Wyler ignored her and secured the undertaker. He double-checked the zip ties of all the men until he was satisfied they would hold. Then he reloaded his crossbow.

"Who else is down here?" Wyler said to the undertaker.

"Fuck you," he replied.

Wyler pressed the tip of the bolt in his crossbow against the undertaker's thigh. "I've three more of these. I'd be more than happy to turn you into a pin cushion."

"Why ... why the fuck did you come back?" Xolo said, coming out of his terrorized state.

Wyler turned to him.

"Yeah, I know it's you," Xolo said smugly. "You and that fucking dog. We're going to kill you. You know that, right? When Tenoch gets back ... we're going to find you and filet you alive."

"Right now, you're batting oh-for-two," Wyler said. "I like my odds."

Xolo spat at Wyler and cursed in Spanish. Wyler returned his attention to the undertaker. "Who else is down here?"

"Don't you fucking answer—" was all Xolo got out before Mya silenced him with a blow from the butt of her crossbow. Blood dripped from his mouth.

"Last chance," Wyler said, pressing the arrow deeper into the undertaker's thigh. He winced, trying to squirm away from the pressure.

"There's one more guy in the arena," the undertaker said.

"That's it?" Wyler said, pressing even harder.

"Yes. Fuck. That's it."

"Do you believe him?" Wyler said to Mya.

Mya crouched in front of the undertaker, then pressed the gun into his neck, holding it there as she studied the man's face. After five seconds, she pulled the gun back and stood.

"Yeah, I believe him."

"Alright, let's keep moving," Wyler said. "Blackjack, on me."

Blackjack broke from his rigid stance in front of Xolo and followed them to the exit.

"You're ... fucking ... dead ..." Xolo mumbled through his busted jaw.

"Maybe," Wyler said over his shoulder as Mya and Blackjack walked out. "But not today."

He stepped into the corridor, closed the door, then smashed the handle with the crossbow butt.

"That got the blood pumping," Mya said, decocking the gun and slipping it into her waistband.

"Appreciate the assist," Wyler said.

"No problem. It's just increasing the size of the favor you're going to owe me."

Wyler grinned. "Don't I know it."

They continued forward, taking a left down the next corridor, and stopped at the entrance to the arena. Wyler carefully peered around the corner. A small pool of light cascaded down to the center ring. No one stood around the perimeter. He waved two

fingers to Mya, and they crept inside, crouching low. At the top
row of seating, Wyler peeked over the edge. A guy, a little older
than Xolo, stood in the center wearing headphones, spraying the
concrete with a hose, oblivious to their presence or what had
happened to his fellow scumbags. Wyler hand signaled to Mya
a plan of attack. She nodded in understanding, then broke off
to the right, continuing to stay low, while Wyler and Blackjack
went left.

The dim lighting masked their approach. Wyler snaked his
way down the stairs on an angle from the guy's direct line of sight.
He waited until Mya was in position. Then she walked straight
to the center of the ring. It took the guy a second to notice her.
When he did, it was too late. Distracted in the front, Wyler snuck
up from behind and put the guy in a sleeper hold. He struggled at
first, digging his nails into Wyler's forearms. But the fight drained
out of him quickly, and his body went limp. Wyler dragged the
guy to the chains used to secure the dogs before the fights. After
binding the guy's hands, Wyler gave a thumbs up to Mya.

"That should be everybody," he said. "How we doing on time?"

She checked her watch. "Five minutes to eleven."

"Alright, final push."

Wyler led the way through the door that connected back to the
training area of the bunker and up the stairs out to the van. Mya
unlocked it and swung open the door. They each took one side
of the duffle bag and went back down. When they arrived at the
kennel, no dogs barked. A promising sign, Wyler thought. It meant
the pills were working. He walked in front of each cage, studying
the dogs. Six of them lay on their sides, eyes closed, breathing
heavily. Two were lying down but had their heads up. Their eyes

were barely open. And the last two were more alert than he expected. They both were still standing and pacing their cages.

"Shouldn't they be out cold right now?" Mya asked.

"Toss me the pills. They're a little bit bigger. Might need an extra dose."

Mya handed Wyler the pills. While he stuffed them into the treats, she unzipped the duffle bag and laid out the harnesses. When Wyler finished, he helped Mya with the rest of the gear.

"So, how are we doing this?" she asked.

"We'll tackle the ones that are fully out first." He picked up a small fabric muzzle. "You open the cage, and I'll slip the muzzle on. Once that's secured, we take the dog out and put them in the harness." Wyler pointed to one of the harnesses on the ground. It was made of thick canvas that folded like a taco, connecting two handles at the top. Essentially, they would take the dogs out like carrying logs to a fireplace. Wyler then pointed to Velcro straps. "Then we bind their feet together. If they wake up it'll restrict their movements. After that, it's hauling them out of here and loading them into the van."

"Guess I'll be getting my workout in for the day," Mya said, cracking her knuckles in preparation for the heavy lifting.

"Set a timer on your watch to get a baseline for how long each dog will take us."

"Alright." Mya tapped on her watch, then said, "Ready."

Wyler took a deep breath. All of his planning led him to this moment. It was another chance for him to prevent what happened to Maximus all those years ago. Wyler looked at Mya. "Hit it."

The timer started. They went to the first cage. Wyler nodded once he was set. Mya pulled back the bolt and eased the cage gate open. The pit bull had a brindle fur pattern. A male on the smaller side compared to some of the others. Wyler gently slipped the muzzle over the dog's head. He felt several hardened scars behind the dog's ears. The dog groaned from being jostled but didn't attempt to get up.

"Bringing him out now," Wyler said.

Blackjack paced behind Wyler, supervising the transfer of his brethren to the harness. Wyler crouched and lifted the dog far enough off the cement floor for Mya to slide the harness underneath. She worked the legs through the holes. Then she quickly wrapped them with Velcro straps like a seasoned rodeo hand.

"Done," she said, passing her handles to Wyler. He latched them, then set them on the floor.

"Perfect," he said. "Next up."

They repeated the process for the second dog, another male pitbull. After lowering it onto the harness, Wyler pulled his hand out and saw it was coated in blood.

"Fuck," Mya said. "They left him in there with an open wound?"

The rage pressed tightly against Wyler's chest, screaming to break free. "Could be. Or it reopened as we pulled him out." Wyler sighed. "We can't waste time on it now. We'll handle it once we're on the road."

Mya's face was tight. Wyler saw the anger in her eyes as well.

"I got this one," Wyler said, standing. "You grab the first one."

The dog wasn't that big. Maybe fifty or sixty pounds, Wyler guessed. But it was sculpted in pure, dense muscle, making it feel like it weighed closer to ninety pounds. Wyler bent at the knees and hefted the dog into his arms. He waited for Mya to do the same, and they hustled out of the room. At the top of the stairs, Wyler was sucking wind. The sun seemed to evaporate the sweat pouring out of him almost instantaneously. Eight more to go, only four more you need to carry, he told his protesting muscles. Wyler climbed into the van, opened the first cage, and settled the dog onto the plush bedding. Then he opened the next one for Mya and assisted in getting the second dog inside.

As they jumped out of the van, Mya wiped the sweat from her forehead and said, "I'm tacking on a spa day to the favor you're going to owe me. Get one of those big, burly Swedish women to rub me down."

Wyler grinned. He appreciated the sarcasm. It always had a way of cutting the tension, no matter how stressful the situation. Almost everyone he ever fought beside employed the tactic. Dark humor was a close cousin to death. When they returned to the kennel, Wyler said "Time?"

Mya checked her watch. "Fifteen minutes and change."

"And what time is it?"

"11:17 AM."

Wyler did the math. Fifteen minutes times four more trips came out to another hour, putting them about fifteen minutes over their two-hour window. It was closer than he wanted. It left no margin for error.

"Let's move it then."

The next two dogs came out, got loaded up, and hauled to the van. With every slow step Wyler took, he heard another second ticking off the clock. Dehydration, the grueling sun, and mental and physical exhaustion all combined into a punishing cocktail. It reminded Wyler of boot camp. Four dogs down, Wyler repeated in his head as he trudged back to the kennel. Four dogs down, six to go. Mya's breathing was as heavy as Wyler's, securing the next two dogs. Remember why you're here. Maximus. Soto. Don't let it all be for nothing. Push. Go. Don't stop. Wyler lifted his third dog. His forearms felt like someone was grinding a radial sander against them. The burns were inflamed and swollen from the continual chafing of the canvas harnesses. He felt his body struggling and slowing down.

When they returned for the next batch of dogs, Wyler said between breaths, "Time?"

"11:55 AM," Mya said as she hunched over, resting her hands on her knees.

They had lost time. At their current rate, they would finish closer to 12:30 PM. Rafa and Tenoch would have figured out by then that the call from the warden was bullshit. Wyler wondered if they would put together that he had anything to do with it. All he could do was hope that they didn't. He looked at Mya.

"Still got gas left in the tank?"

"Always." She forced a smile. "When I get home, I think I'm going to need to dust off the treadmill."

They exchanged an exhausted laugh. Then Wyler nudged her in the arm with his elbow.

"Come on. We've only got four left."

Mya grunted. "Only four left, he says."

She opened the next cage, and Wyler repeated the process. When the eighth dog was secured, they headed for the van. Wyler's feet felt like they were trudging through hardening cement. To make matters worse, the dog in his arms wasn't entirely out. It squirmed against the restraints. The motion renewed the pain washing over Wyler's skin.

"Easy," he said to the dog, fighting to maintain his balance. "Easy, boy, easy."

After loading the dog in the van, Wyler stepped into the heat. His vision doubled, then darkened. He steadied himself against the door.

"Shit. You alright?" Mya said, hopping out of the van.

"I'm good."

"You don't look good. Let me get some water."

"We don't have time."

"And I won't have time to try and hoist your ass into the van if you black out." She popped into the van and returned with a jug of water. "Now drink."

The water was warm but refreshing nonetheless. Wyler alternated between taking sips and pouring it over his head.

"Those arms of yours look like shit, too," Mya said after chugging some water.

"I'll live." He took another swig of water and tossed the jug back into the van. It gave him enough of a boost to finish the job. "Break time's over."

Two more, he told himself. Two more, and you'll have completed what you set out to do. Ten dogs that will have a life that otherwise wouldn't. Ten dogs that won't have to suffer. He held onto the thought and pushed forward.

The second to last dog came out with no issues. When Mya went to open the last cage, the pit bull lunged at her.

"Jesus," she said, snatching her hand back. She studied it as if to ensure she still had all her fingers. "How the fuck is he still standing?"

"Good question. Either he's got a tolerance to the meds, or he's hopped up on another drug."

"Like what?"

Wyler shrugged. "I've heard they sometimes give them a shot of cocaine, but who knows."

"So what do you want to do?"

"I'll give him one more small dose. I don't want to go too far in the opposite direction, especially if something else is in his system. Don't need his heart stopping. You take this one and wait for me in the van. As soon as I can move him, I'll come up, and we'll get the hell out of here."

"You sure?"

"Yeah," Wyler said. "And if anything should happen, just get these dogs to Arlo."

"You think I'm going to leave you here? No way," Mya said, shaking her head. "'Leave no man behind.' Remember that motto?"

Wyler nodded, knowing further arguments would fall on deaf ears. "I guess I'll see you soon then."

"I fucking better."

Wyler helped Mya hoist the dog into her arms. Once she disappeared around the corner, Wyler took out the pills and treats. He put a half dose inside and dropped it into the cage. The dog ate it willingly. Wyler checked the time on his phone. 12:25 PM. There was no sign of trouble yet, but that didn't mean it wasn't around the corner. For all he knew, a SWAT team or a gang of cartel members were about to come crashing in. With a few minutes to kill, Wyler got to work on the last part of his plan.

When Wyler first decided to come back for the dogs, he saw the inherent problem with just taking them. It left the possibility for no one to know what happened there and for Tenoch to get more dogs and start again. For Wyler, that was an unacceptable outcome. Rafa's operation needed to be shut down permanently. And he had a good idea of how to do it.

Chapter 18

Wyler looped a chain around the door handle leading into the training room. He tied the tail end to one of the cages, pinning the door open. From the medical supply cabinet, he found a bottle of rubbing alcohol and a towel. He dumped the entire contents onto the towel until it was fully saturated. With his fuse primed, Wyler went into the training facility. At the oven near the propane tanks, he cut open the tubes that fed the machine. Then he cranked the knobs, turning them on. A hiss came from the nozzles as the gas pumped out. Wyler estimated there was enough propane to blow through the ceiling and level at least half the training facility and kennel. An explosion of that size would be difficult for Rafa to cover up. There would be questions. People would investigate. Rafa couldn't silence them all.

Muffled grunts came from behind Wyler. He turned and saw the first guy they encountered coming into the bunker. The guy pulled on his restraints as if he understood what Wyler was doing. Few, Wyler guessed, would blame him if he left the guy to his fate. But Wyler didn't want that blood on his hands if he could avoid it.

"Don't try anything," Wyler said to the guy as he pulled out the gun with his right hand and the knife with his left. "Nod, if you understand me."

The guy hesitated, then nodded and mumbled through his gag. Wyler cut the connecting zip tie.

"Nice and slow now," Wyler said, motioning with the gun for the guy to stand up. "We're going to the arena." Blackjack stuck close to Wyler's side. "If you run, he'll drag you down again. Understand?"

Another nod and grunt. Wyler continually scanned the facility. An uneasiness rippled up his spine that he was out of time. The ticking of the clock wouldn't leave him alone. His heavy breathing filled the empty spaces between each tick.

When they reached the door to the arena, Wyler said, "Open it."

The guy hesitated and tilted his head slightly as if he were trying to look at Wyler without turning around. The movement was subtle but revealing. The guy was going to make a move. Wyler's muscles tensed in anticipation. Then, as soon as the guy crossed the threshold, he spun and tried to slam the door closed. Wyler wedged his shoe into the space between the frame, preventing it from shutting. The guy grunted through his gag and bounced on the door, desperately trying to close it. He didn't have time for this.

"Get ready," he said to Blackjack.

Wyler planted his left foot, crouched, leaned back, and gave the door one good ram with his shoulder. He held the opening just long enough for Blackjack to slip through. "Go. Go. Go."

Blackjack slithered through like water through a crack. Two seconds later, the pressure on the door gave way, and Wyler spilled into the arena. The guy shook his leg, trying to kick Blackjack loose. While he was distracted, Wyler walked up behind him. Using the butt of the gun, he struck the guy in the back of the head, sending him unconscious to the ground.

"Release," Wyler said, pulling Blackjack off. Wyler tucked the gun into his waistband and dragged the body next to the other tied-up guy. After securing him, he and Blackjack hustled back to the kennel. His phone read 12:35 PM. Another ten minutes gone. His heart was working on overdrive after the scuffle. It slammed against his ribs like a hammer trying to break concrete. The bunker walls felt like they were closing in on him. He preferred operations that were quick-hitting. Thirty minutes max. Clocking in at over two and a half hours was an eternity. Every wasted minute allowed enemy forces to regroup and send in a fresh attack. At two and a half hours, the element of surprise was long gone.

The last dog was finally lying down, but his head remained upright. The pit bull panted as it glared at Wyler. Hatred filled the dog's eyes. Wyler could only imagine the horrors the dog had been subjected to. He would've liked the dog completely out, but time was up.

"Alright, boy," Wyler said, opening the gate. "I'm going to get you out of here, okay."

Wyler crept his hand forward with the muzzle. The dog snapped at him. "Easy. Easy. I know you've had a rough go of things. I'm not here to hurt you."

The dog struggled to his feet and then collapsed. Wyler motioned to Blackjack. "Come here."

Blackjack came to Wyler's side and sniffed inside the cage. The pit bull growled.

"Easy," Wyler said, lowering his voice and projecting a calm energy. "We're friends. It's going to be okay."

Blackjack inched closer, putting his snout up to the pit bulls. Both dogs tensed. Then the pit bull sniffed back at Blackjack. It was the sign he was looking for. They were establishing a hierarchy and showing they weren't a threat. Wyler slowly reached his hand inside and touched the dog's side. When the dog didn't react, Wyler gently ran his hand over the fur. One wrong move, and the dog could clamp onto his arm. Prying it loose would be next to impossible. Wyler's instincts told him to forgo another attempt with the muzzle. He pulled out a treat and crouched in front of the harness. The pit bull perked up, seeing the food.

"Ready to go?" Wyler said, waving the treat.

The pit bull hesitated, then slowly got to his feet. He wobbled out of the cage and stopped on the harness. Wyler dropped the treat to the ground. As the dog ate it, Wyler slipped the harness over his legs and quickly closed the two ends together. He exhaled a long sigh, having secured the final dog. The last thing he had to do was light the fuse and get the hell out of there.

Wyler grabbed the alcohol-drenched rag and ran to the opposite door leading into the kennel. He fished a lighter from his pocket, flicked it to life, and tapped the flame against the rag. After it burst into a fiery blaze, Wyler dropped it and ran back to the pit bull. Last push, dig deep, move, he told himself. He scooped the dog into his arms. Before taking his first step, a voice shouted out behind him.

"Don't move!"

Wyler's stomach twisted. His heart thundered. The muscles

in his legs froze. He sensed a gun was trained on him.

"Why don't you turn around," the voice said. "Nice and slow."

Wyler did as instructed. Standing in the doorway was a guy dressed in a tailored suit. He was about Wyler's height, with perfectly groomed hair. The glint of a badge attached to his belt peeked out from beneath the blazer. And the blocky shape of the gun in his hand, a Glock, confirmed for Wyler he was staring at a cop.

At 12:05 PM, Amos's secondary phone vibrated. He walked outside before answering it.

"You called?" It was Tenoch.

"Yeah," Amos said. "Where are you?"

"California. What do you want?"

"I had a sighting of our guy. He was staying at a motel up in the northeastern part of the city. He spotted me and took off into the desert." Amos paused, inhaling, then said, "I lost him out there."

Silence. Then, "You lost him?"

"The car couldn't handle the terrain. I had to turn back. But there's only so many places he could have gone." Amos waited for a reprimand of some kind, but none came, just more silence. "You still there?"

"Something's not right," Tenoch finally said.

"What do you mean?"

"Rafa got a call yesterday from the warden in San Quentin about his uncle. He said it was urgent and that Rafa should talk to him in person to discuss. But his uncle was fine when we arrived, and the warden had no idea what we were talking about."

Amos took the comb from his pocket and ran his thumb over the smooth plastic teeth, thinking. "Someone faked the call?

Why?" Then he stopped rubbing the comb. "You think it's the same guy, Wyler, behind it?"

"I don't know. If you said he's still in Vegas, then it's possible."

"But why? What would he have to gain by getting you out of the state? What if it's Agosti making another play?"

"Again, I don't fucking know. This is what I thought we were paying you for. To get us answers to questions like this."

Amos ran the comb through his hair to keep his temper in check. He had nothing to do with the Wyler situation happening. And he was the one who advised them not to make the bet with Agosti. As far as Amos was concerned, this was Tenoch's problem. For him to get pissy—he didn't finish the thought. It wouldn't do him any good arguing with the man. If anything, it just gave him more leverage for the future.

"So what do you want me to do?" Amos said, putting the comb away.

"Go to the house. Check it out. Make sure nothing is going on there."

"Why would something be going on there?"

"Because no one answered when I tried calling the coliseum. I know my guys. That's not like them. They always answer."

Amos couldn't explain why Wyler was still in Vegas, but he didn't see him as someone breaking into Rafa's house or bunker. To him, a thug from Agosti's camp made more sense. Wyler had nothing to gain, but Agosti did. Either way, it didn't really matter. Checking out the house couldn't hurt.

"Alright, I can swing by there," Amos said. "Should I take backup?"

"No. Keep this quiet as long as you can. It's probably nothing, but we can't take any chances now."

If Agosti sent men, Amos didn't love being alone but understood the need for discretion.

"I'll head out now," Amos said.

"We're getting on a flight at 1 PM. We should be back a little after three. I want a debrief after that."

The phone went dead. Amos sighed as he put the phone away. This better be fucking worth it, he thought.

At the police station lot, the attendant smirked at Amos as he held the keys back. "Think you can handle not destroying another one?"

"Wow, that's original," Amos said, rolling his eyes. "You can take that act onto the *Tonight Show*."

"I know it's not as funny as your driving skills," the attendant laughed.

"Give me the goddamn keys."

The attendant slid them over. "Sorry, I'm fresh out of helmets for you."

Amos ignored the remark, snatched the keys, and walked off. He fired up the new car and headed for Rafa's. His mind drifted to what he might find. He guessed nothing, but if there was something ... he'd handle it like he always did. Fifteen minutes later, he stopped at the gate. After checking his rearview, Amos swiped his access card across the face of the intercom device. The monitor beeped, then the gate opened. He parked on the street in front of the house. From the outside, everything was quiet. He knew better than to read too much into the slumbering appearance. At the front door, he drew his Glock, swiped the card again, and entered.

He stood still, listening. Nothing. Amos moved forward with his gun raised as if someone would jump out from around a corner any second. His senses tuned into the surroundings, alert to anything unusual. He cleared the first floor, then the basement. Again nothing. He relaxed slightly when he got to the second floor and found everything as it should be. As he was about to leave the master bedroom, a glint of light caught his eye in the distance. Amos went to the window, where he could just see the top of an object jutting out from behind a rise in the landscape. It was too far away for him to confirm what it was.

He hustled down the stairs and went out the back door. Whatever he saw, it was near the bunker. Maybe Tenoch was right after all, Amos thought. He didn't remember Rafa keeping cash in the coliseum. What would anyone be there for? The only thing of value was the dogs. As Amos got closer, he could tell the object he saw from the house was part of a vehicle. Someone was definitely there and had knowledge of the bunker. He debated whether to go to the vehicle first or inside the bunker. If it was Agosti's crew with the vehicle, Amos guessed he'd be outmanned and outgunned. If he went into the bunker first—and Tenoch's guys were still alive—then that gave him reinforcements to take on anyone else. But then he thought about what Tenoch said about his guys not answering. Did they not answer because they'd all been slaughtered? The prospect didn't fill him with confidence. He almost called in backup but resisted the urge. They probably wouldn't get there in time anyway. Besides, he needed to think of a story to spin for being there. The decision was made then. He'd go into the bunker first.

Amos went down the narrow passage leading to the entrance. His card unlocked the heavy metal door. The lights flickered on as he entered. His breathing sped up. He hated the place. Something about being underground always spooked him. He had an irrational fear the ceiling would cave in, trapping him alive and leading to a long, drawn-out death. He shook the thought away and continued down the hallway. At the juncture, he could go left or right. Since the dogs were the only real thing of value, if anyone was in the bunker, he guessed they'd be there. At each turn, he pressed his back to the wall, then spun out with his gun leveled, ready to drop anyone who fell into his sights. When he reached the door, Amos steadied his breathing and leaned in. He couldn't hear anything through the thick door.

Before entering, he wiped the sweat from his hands. Then he gripped the handle and barged in. Seeing someone inside momentarily shocked him into paralysis. He was grateful whoever it was had their back to him.

"Don't move!" he shouted, regaining his wits and putting the sights of his gun center mass. "Why don't you turn around. Nice and slow."

When the guy turned, Amos motioned at his face.

"Lose the mask."

The man shifted the dog's weight to one arm while he used his other hand to pull down the bandana. Something akin to glee fluttered through Amos's chest. He recognized Declan Wyler from the security footage at the hotel.

"Son of a bitch," Amos said, grinning. "It must be my lucky day."

His finger tightened around the trigger. He almost squeezed off a round but stopped. Wyler was dead to rights. Why add a body to his record when he didn't have to? Tenoch will be back soon. Let him handle it. Prevents Tenoch from having dirt on him while simultaneously completing the job asked of him. Amos smiled, knowing he would be one step closer to getting what he wanted. And it was all thanks to the man standing in front of him.

When the gun didn't fire, Wyler exhaled. Not getting shot on the spot meant something. So either Tenoch still wanted him alive, or he wanted to do the killing himself. Either way, it gave Wyler a chance. He just needed to stall long enough to cash it in.

"Who're you?" Wyler asked.

"That's not important," Amos replied. "Why don't you put the dog down."

"You know who I am."

"Why do you say that?"

Wyler shrugged. "Were you the one following me this morning?"

"Yeah. And now I won't hear the end of it at work. That joyride really messed up my car."

Wyler stifled a smile. He was happy his plan had worked. "How did you find me?"

"I have my methods."

"How long have you been on Ortega's payroll?"

"I work for the city of Las Vegas. And you're trespassing on private property, clearly in the midst of a burglary."

"So, am I under arrest?"

The grin that widened on the cop's face said plenty. It made the hairs on Wyler's forearms stand up. Blackjack growled and stepped forward. When the gun swung in his direction, Wyler said, "Easy."

"If that dog moves again, I will empty my magazine into him. Then I'm going to reload and do the same to you."

"He won't move unless I tell him to."

"That's good. Put the dog down."

Wyler crouched and gently laid the pit bull on the ground. He didn't stand. He felt the pressure of the gun at his hip. One distraction, and he could go for it.

"So, let me get this straight," Amos said. "Instead of getting paid to train these dogs to fight, you tell Ortega to fuck off. Then you almost get killed, escape, and almost get killed again. That was your handy work at the hotel, right?"

Wyler shrugged.

"And then, instead of running for it like any normal person would," Amos continued. "You come back to the same place where you were almost killed the first time to steal some dogs? Do I have that right?"

Wyler didn't respond, focusing on going for the gun. He visualized each movement.

Amos shook his head. "I don't get it. Are you one of those animal rights pussies or something? Why risk your life for some meaningless dogs?"

"Their lives aren't meaningless to me."

"Jesus, buddy, you sound like a five-year-old. You know you're not leaving this place alive, right? You're telling me a dog was worth that?"

"Guess so," Wyler said, shrugging again. Then he nodded at the burning rag, readying to make his move. "If you don't put that out soon, neither of us will leave here alive."

The grin vanished from the cop's face. This was the opportunity Wyler needed.

"What are you talking about?" Amos said, aiming the gun back at Wyler.

"You smell that?" Wyler watched closely as the cop sniffed the air and then glanced at the burning rag. "I opened the tanks used to fuel the oven in the other room. When the gas hits that flame, we go out in a blaze of glory. I figure you've got less than five minutes."

"Bull shit."

"You keep waiting; you'll find out soon enough." Wyler stared into the cop's eyes. "I was willing to give my life for these dogs. Are you?"

When Wyler spotted the panic seep into the cop's face, he knew the next few seconds would happen quickly. The cop finally broke his gaze on Wyler, scanning the room for a way to put out the fire. Not seeing any, he turned to the small blaze. That was when Wyler made his move.

He sprang to his right, staying low, pulling out the gun. The cop saw the movement and opened fire. The shots went wild, with his attention split. Wyler landed on the floor and squeezed the trigger three times in rapid succession. The second bullet hit the cop in the gut, doubling him over. The cop staggered past the fire and fell behind the first waist-high divider walls. Wyler fired another three rounds as he scrambled to his feet. His adrenaline surged on full throttle.

"Blackjack, on me," Wyler shouted.

Wyler fired again, keeping the cop pinned behind the wall, as Blackjack ran over. Once he was behind him, Wyler said, "Go. Outside. Now." Blackjack kept running and disappeared into the training facility. Wyler fired a single round every few seconds while sidestepping back to the pit bull. With his left hand, he grabbed the harness handle. He started backpedaling, dragging the dog toward the door with the gun aimed at where the cop hid. Then he heard a whooshing noise, and the flame brightened. A scream followed—an awful, terrified scream. The cop stumbled out from behind the wall, his arms flailing. His pant leg was engulfed in flames. He swatted frantically at the orange wave rushing upward.

A lump of fear swelled in Wyler's throat as he reached the training facility. The smell of gas was overpowering. And now, with a more considerable fire burning, he had even less time to get out before the explosion. When Wyler cleared the door frame, he dropped the gun and scooped up the dog. His legs didn't respond to the commands telling them to run. He was spent. Any second, the flames would kiss the gas. Keep going, he told himself. Don't stop. He felt like he was moving on a conveyor belt, going in the wrong direction. The door to freedom and safety never seemed to get closer. At least Blackjack had made it out, he thought next. Mya would give him a good life. And you saved nine out of the ten dogs. Not bad. No. Stop it. He expelled the idea of defeat from his mind and barrelled forward. His arms were loose rubber bands trying to hold up what felt like the weight of a car.

Ten feet remained. Six feet, then three. He was going to make it, his heart determined. As soon as Wyler reached the door, he kicked out the wedge that propped it open. When his foot touched the first step, the gas ignited.

Chapter 19

A wave of hot air blasted Wyler into the stairwell, slamming the door shut behind him. He turned just enough to not land on top of the pit bull. His shoulder collided with the cement steps, sending a blinding pain down the right side of his body. The impact knocked the air from his lungs. A vibration radiated through him and the ground like an electrical current. A ringing in his ears drowned out the sounds of earth and chunks of the stairwell raining down from above. He shielded his head with his left arm while using his body to block the debris from hitting the dog. All he could do was close his eyes and hope the stairwell didn't collapse. It reminded Wyler of a time when his platoon was shelled by Iraqi forces. Fear left his body as a cool haze enveloped him. There was an odd comfort in having the decision of whether he lived or died taken out of his control. Waiting and doing nothing was all he could do. There was peace in that.

Gradually, the raining debris slowed, and the ringing faded. The stairwell had held. Wyler did a mental scan of his body before attempting to move. His shoulder hurt, his ribs throbbed, and his skin burned, but none of the injuries felt life-threatening. After twenty seconds of lying there, Wyler felt something warm and coarse on his fingers. He opened his eyes and looked up. A dusty Blackjack stood on the steps licking Wyler's hand. A tan cloud of earth blocked out the blue sky. Wyler smiled at Blackjack as he scratched the dog's head.

"Good boy," Wyler croaked. His mouth was dry, and his throat ached.

"Jesus, Wyler," Mya shouted next. "What the fuck happened?"

She picked her way through the crumbling stairwell and stopped at his side.

"Didn't want them ... doing it again," Wyler said.

"Would a little warning have killed you? I damn near shit myself."

"Okay ... new underwear ... is on me."

Mya helped him up. Together, they hoisted the last pit bull out. Topside, Wyler surveyed the damage. To his left, the flat desert had transformed into a forty-yard-wide crater. Smoke billowed through some of the fissures created on the desert floor. A sickening smell of burnt chemicals hung heavy in the air. Dust floated through the breeze, looking for a place to resettle.

"Come on," Mya said. "Let's load this guy in and get out of here. Half the fucking city probably heard that blast."

Mya opened the door. Wyler and Blackjack got in the back while Mya climbed behind the wheel. Once Wyler loaded the pit bull into his bed, he said, "Hit it."

The van accelerated, slow at first, then picked up speed. Wyler looked out the window, watching the smoke fade into the distance. He'd done his job. Someone would find Soto now, and his body could rest in peace. Wyler wondered how long it would take him to be able to do the same.

He found the jug of water, took a long drink, then poured some onto a towel. After wiping himself down, he dropped into the passenger seat. Mya drove north, sticking to the desert instead of the main roads in case of any police roadblocks. When they cleared the city, she cut east until they crossed into Arizona. During that time, Wyler attended to the dogs while they were still sedated. All but one of them had scars over their bodies. Some of which were fresher than others. A few were missing teeth, and some had damage to their eyes. What internal wounds they suffered from would be determined at Arlo's. The same went for whatever psychological pain they had endured. Wyler then removed the muzzles from each dog and put food and water inside for when they woke up. They had about a five-day drive ahead of them to get to Virginia. Wyler had enough of the pills to keep them mildly sedated for the length of the trip.

After twenty minutes into Arizona, Mya merged onto the I-15 and continued on it into Utah.

"What do you say we stop at a hotel to regroup? Shower, eat, get a few hours of sleep before setting off."

It sounded like Christmas come early to Wyler. He figured they were far enough from Las Vegas, and being in a new state would provide them with jurisdictional safety. The cops were looking for Wyler and a Bronco. Not Mya and a van. He also assumed it would take whatever agencies showed up at Rafa's to piece things together and tie him to it—if they did at all.

"It's a good idea," Wyler said.

Ten minutes later, Mya pulled into the lot of a Hampton Inn. She went in, came back out, and leaned in through the window.

"We're all set. And you're in luck; the place is pet-friendly."

Wyler staggered out of the van, and Blackjack followed. Dust plumed off them as they hit the pavement. Mya reached inside the van and hit a switch.

"I used the same solar panel technology that I put on your Bronco. The panels on the roof feed into the battery system under the floor. So it'll run the auxiliary air conditioning unit while we're inside."

"You got to patent that. Can get on *Shark Tank*."

"Pfft. *Shark Tank* is for amateurs. And who says I haven't already started the patent process?"

Wyler held up his hands. "Excuse me for implying anything contradictory to your business prowess."

Mya grinned. "Apology accepted."

The three of them wearily trekked up to their room. It was small but clean, with a single queen bed.

"I can go get us some food if you want to shower first," Wyler said.

"Works for me."

Wyler left and found a sandwich shop within walking distance of the hotel. When he returned, Mya was showered, in fresh clothes, and in the process of fixing her hair. She was a sight to behold. After Wyler hosed off, dried, and brushed Blackjack, he showered. His shoulder throbbed, but he didn't think anything was broken or dislodged. The cold water soothed his chafed skin. He downed four Tynelols in the shower, then got out. The three ate their sandwiches silently, each decompressing from the day's chaos. When they finished, Mya flopped onto the bed. Blackjack hopped up and curled into a ball.

"I'll take the floor," Wyler said.

Mya slapped the spot next to her on the bed. "Don't be an idiot. Lay down."

"You sure?"

"Yeah, just don't get handsy."

"Same goes for you."

He was asleep two seconds after his head hit the pillow.

Mya gently shook him awake.

"We should go," she said.

Wyler sat up, feeling like he could use another week of sleep. "What time is it?"

"Six."

A three-hour nap. It wasn't much, but he knew it was better than nothing. Wyler collected their stuff and went to the van while Mya checked them out.

"Got some disapproving looks from the concierge," Mya said with a grin, getting into the van.

"Oh, yeah?"

"Think she thought we were here for a torrid rendezvous."

"For three hours? That's some rendezvous."

Mya laughed. "Fucking Utah."

She shifted into gear and settled into the seat, getting comfortable for the thirty-five hour, twenty-three hundred mile drive ahead. Wyler slept for another three hours and woke up halfway into Arizona. He checked on the dogs again. Half of them were awake but still in a semi-drugged state. They would need to stop periodically throughout the trip to let them out and clean down the cages. It would be a process, but not impossible. At the six-hour mark, they crossed the border into New Mexico.

"You ready to switch?" Wyler asked.

"I'm good for a little longer if you talk to me."

"Alright. You got a topic in mind?"

"Something good. Something to get my blood pumping."

Wyler smiled. "Such as?"

"Tell me about your love life."

"Wow, so not starting small. No easing in?"

"We're friends. We don't need to start small or 'ease in.' This isn't a first date. Shit. What, you want to talk about the weather first? It's hot. The end. Come on. Give me something juicy. You still seeing what's her face? Ebony?"

"Enola," Wyler said. "And no."

"Okay. Now we're on to something. What happened?"

He shrugged.

"Come on, out with it," Mya said, swatting him in the arm.

Wyler hesitated, then said, "She wanted to focus on her work, and I was a distraction. So I left and gave her space."

"But ..."

"What do you mean, but?"

"I know there's more. You can't summarize a break up in two sentences."

"I thought that's what I just did."

"Don't make me slap you again."

"You really want to hear about this?"

"Yes. My heart is racing already with the mystery and intrigue."

Wyler sighed as he looked out the window. His reluctance came from a similar fear he had with Ellie. He didn't care what strangers thought of him, but for those few who were close to him, their views mattered. If anyone would understand, though, it would be Mya.

"When I got Blackjack, I was doing a favor for Arlo," Wyler started. "Dogs being bred for a life in the military were disappearing from a breeder's farm. It took me three days to find the guys responsible. Two heroin addicts were stealing the dogs and selling them for drug money. Things happened, and … let's just say neither of them walk this earth anymore."

"Jesus. So much for easing in," Mya said.

"You want me to stop?"

"I didn't say that."

Wyler continued, "I was with Enola during and after that. We raised Blackjack together. Taught him a lot of what he knows. One night, I had a little too much to drink, and I implied what happened to the two addicts." Wyler scratched his chin. "And now that I'm in a new relationship, I can't help but look back on the old one. And I wonder if the whole focusing on her work was just an excuse. I revealed who I was and what I can do … and maybe Enola realized she didn't like what she saw."

Mya paused before saying, "It's possible. Telling someone you've … ended some lives, even if they're pieces of shit, can have that effect on regular people."

"I know."

"And so you haven't said anything to this new chick?"

"Right."

"But she asks?"

"Not in so many words. But she can tell I'm holding back." Wyler looked at Mya. "You've been with Naomi for how long now?"

"A little over a year on and off and full on for the last two years."

"And you told her what you were doing here with me?"

"Fuck no," Mya said, then laughed. "Are you nuts?"

Wyler frowned and returned to looking out the window.

"Sorry," Mya said. "I didn't mean to come off like that. She knows mostly about what I did overseas in the military. Things I've done post that, back home, here in the States, not so much. But it's different though. That's her, you know what I mean? She couldn't handle all that. But you're a poker player. You make a living off of reading people. What's your impression of this new girl?" Mya shook her head again. "And listen to me, 'new girl.' What's her name?"

"Ellie. Ellie Sloan."

"And backing up—do you want to tell her all your dark bits?"

"Shouldn't I want to?"

"I guess it depends on where you see the relationship going. If this is just a fling and you can't picture being with her long-term, then yeah, I don't know that I'd get too far into the weeds of your past. But if you see this as the whole happily ever after type of dream with a house, kids, and all that shit, then I could see you considering it. That's really the question you need to answer before anything."

"Yeah," Wyler said.

He loved Ellie despite never saying the words to her face yet. He got the sense she felt the same. They had a good thing going. Would telling her about his past ruin all of that? Or would it pull them closer together if she accepted him, ugly parts and all? Was that the ultimate test of commitment? No secrets. Build their relationship on a foundation of trust. Then Wyler thought of Enola. He'd loved her too. She wasn't easy to let go of. Was he just trying to fill that void with Ellie, or was she 'the one'? Or was he meant to be alone? Did the fact that he took people's lives some-how automatically rule him out of that type of happiness? These were all questions he didn't love thinking about. Wyler tried to live life simply. Relationships had a way of creating complications.

"So, what's she look like?" Mya said. "This Ellie Sloan. The name sounds sexy. Is she sexy? Describe her for me in detail. Don't leave anything out."

Wyler laughed. He appreciated her trying to lighten the mood.

"You're sick, you know that?" Wyler said.

"What'd I do? Is it wrong that I love the female form?"

"Yet men are the ones who get labeled as dirtbags."

Mya grinned. "Well, you are, but I admit there's some benefits to being a woman."

"I'd call you a dog, but that'd be an insult to dogs."

She laughed, then glanced at Wyler. Her tone turned sincere. "You'll figure it out. I said it before and I'll say it again, trust your gut. It's got you this far in life. Don't stop listening to it now."

Wyler nodded. "Thanks."

"Now, let me see some photos of her," Mya said. "Racier, the better."

For the remainder of the trip, Wyler and Mya rotated the driving shifts into six-hour increments, stopping only for gas, food, and to let the dogs out. A day and a half later, the van approached the Blackstone Dog Sanctuary in rural Virginia. It was run by Wyler's friend, Arlo Riggins—a former Marine with a near prodigy-like mind for numbers. After Arlo left the service, he worked the Wall Street scene for a few years before opening his own brokerage firm. His hard work and understanding of the markets led him to recently earn the rare moniker of a billionaire. Like Wyler, he grew up with a deep love for dogs, and once he had the financial means, he built the Blackstone sanctuary. It occupied nearly fifty acres of land. An old frontier-style fence surrounded the entirety of the property, secured by state-of-the-art security cameras and sensors. Much of the technology came from the advances implemented at the southern border. Regarding security, Arlo never scrimped on shelling out the big bucks.

With Mya behind the wheel, she drove under the arch, serving as the entrance to the vast estate. The paved road wound through a dense forest until it opened to the main patch of cleared land housing the facilities. Mya braked in front of a sturdier gate enclosing twenty acres of wilderness. Wyler leaned across her and waved at the camera attached to the intercom. Twenty seconds later, the gate slowly opened. The road led to a massive house where Arlo and the people who ran the facilities lived. Like everything Arlo did, the house was designed with meticulous precision. The architects who built it employed every piece of modern knowledge about sustainability. Power came from solar roofing and a dedicated wind farm located west of the property, which created enough energy to sustain every building. Geothermal devices heated and cooled each structure. And a large satellite dish kept them connected to the outside world.

Behind the house were two other large, sustainably constructed, and thought-through buildings. One was a dedicated greenhouse that produced enough food year-round to feed all the staff and the dogs that came into the sanctuary. The other served as a hospital, research lab, training facility, and dog housing quarters. Beyond that, another two-acre plot where the dogs roamed free was fenced in.

"Park over there," Wyler said, pointing to the building that housed the hospital. After Mya killed the engine, they stiffly exited the van.

Arlo appeared from the main house a minute later and headed toward them. He wore dark jeans and a light-colored polo shirt. Arlo walked with a limp and a cane after losing his foot to an IED in Afghanistan. A white and black speckled border collie trotted alongside him.

"How was the drive?" Arlo said.

"I was stuck in tight quarters with a man and eleven dogs for thirty hours," Mya said. "I've had more luxurious trips, let's put it that way."

Arlo smiled, then held his hand out toward the mansion. "Head inside. Someone will see to all your pampering needs to wash away the trauma of your travels."

"Don't listen to her," Wyler said. "She loved every minute of it."

Mya rolled her eyes, then gave Arlo a light kiss on the cheek. "Great to see you again, Arlo. Once I'm clean, we can have a civilized conversation."

"I look forward to it," he said.

As she left, Arlo waved to the hospital, motioning for the staff to help unload the van. Wyler surveyed the three men and two women headed over.

"She's not here," Arlo said. Wyler knew who he meant, but pretended otherwise. "Enola's giving a speech at a conference in San Francisco."

Wyler suppressed a sigh of relief. The last time he saw her left a hole of nostalgia in his heart that he didn't have the energy to deal with again.

"I was surprised to get your call," Arlo said. "I wasn't sure if, after Florida, you'd be getting involved with something like this again."

"It wasn't the plan, trust me." Wyler shifted his focus to his hands. Asking for help didn't come naturally to him. He only did it when he saw no other options. Hence reaching out to Mya. And now he had to do it again with Arlo. "Stuff got hairy out there. Any chance the … resources … you used to cover my tracks in Florida are open to some more work?"

"Let's hear it," Arlo said. "Take it from the top."

Wyler hadn't told Arlo much over the phone when he called three days ago, so he started at the beginning. He detailed Soto's story to get him out to Vegas, how it was mostly a lie, and its fallout with Rafa and Tenoch. He covered his escape, the encounter with Javier, the chase with the cop, and the explosion at the bunker. When Wyler finished, Arlo stayed quiet for a moment. He had a way about him of analyzing any situation without judgment. His analytical mind processed all the possible issues and created ways to solve them in seconds.

"I'll get someone on it," Arlo said. "Initial thoughts, the bunker shouldn't give you any issues. With a body in a grave, an explosion, and remnants of a dog fighting ring, this guy Ortega is going to have plenty to deal with. And it won't exactly help their defense by admitting they tried to kill you twice. So I doubt they'll mention you." Arlo shifted on his cane. "As far as the guy at the hotel … it was self-defense, and whether or not they can even tie that to you is questionable at best. My guess is Ortega's defense lawyers will try to keep it as a suicide. And the assault charge didn't actually happen, so getting that cleared shouldn't prove too difficult."

It was a frank assessment that left Wyler not reassured—reassured wasn't the right word for it. He didn't want to feel reassured that he'd get away with murder, even if it was self-defense and the guy had it coming to him. Closure was maybe a better word to describe how he felt. It would allow him to move forward.

"I appreciate it," Wyler said. They shook hands. Then Arlo pulled an envelope from his back pocket and handed it to Wyler.

"Here," Arlo said.

"What's this?"

"Payment for the dogs."

Wyler peeled back a corner flap of the envelope. He caught the eye of Ben Franklin staring back at him. At least thirty grand. "You didn't hire me this time."

"I know, but that doesn't make any difference. You brought dogs. Everyone here will work to train said dogs, and then they'll be placed with good homes at astronomical prices. That's your cut. Same as last time."

"Uh huh," Wyler said, glancing skeptically at Arlo. "Feels a bit like another ploy to get me to work here again."

"Interpret it how you want," Arlo shrugged. "You'll come back when you're ready."

"You sound pretty sure of that."

"Analyzing people and the decisions they'll make is my job."

"Makes you sound more like a fortune teller than a stock-broker."

"They're not mutually exclusive." Arlo held his arms out wide, gesturing at the landscape. "It's built all this, hasn't it?"

Wyler nodded.

The staff arrived at the van. Arlo gave them instructions and stepped aside. The team strapped on protective gloves and worked methodically to unload the dogs. Most of them were still groggy from the drugs. They blinked into the sun and staggered along with the techs.

"We've settled ten of the greyhounds from Florida," Arlo said.

"They've come a long way. These ones will too. Will it be an uphill battle? Yes, but that's the type of challenge we thrive on here."

Wyler watched as the last dog was unloaded. He knew Arlo was right. Dogs were resilient. They'd come around with the right amount of care and attention. And the sanctuary was the best place possible for that. Wyler felt a heaviness drift off his shoulders. He'd lost a friend and come close to dying himself, but the dogs were safe. At the end of the day, that was what mattered.

"So, will you stay the night?" Arlo asked as he turned and started toward the mansion.

"If you think you can find some room," Wyler said, grinning.

"I think there's a storage closet I can clear out for you."

They both laughed.

"What's next for you after this?" Arlo said.

"I owe someone a vacation."

Arlo arched an eyebrow. "Someone ... easy on the eyes?"

"Not you, too," Wyler groaned.

"Where are you thinking of going?"

Wyler brushed his fingers over his inflamed skin. "I'm thinking somewhere cold."

"Alaska's nice for that in about three months."

Wyler wondered how Ellie would feel about the location. The thought of spending time with her in a cabin by a fire with nowhere to be brought a smile to his face. It took him a little by surprise at the sudden realization of how much he missed her. He put his hands in his pockets and looked at Arlo. "And there's one more favor I have to ask."

"Name it."

"I'm going to need a ride home."

Chapter 20

The sea breeze enveloped Wyler as he leaned against the brick wall of the Whitmore Club. Blackjack sat in an upright pose at his side. Together, they watched the odd assortment of people still roaming the Atlantic City boardwalk at two in the morning. Wyler rolled his lucky chip across his knuckles as a drunken bachelorette party swayed past. The girls hooted and laughed, filled with life and the promise of tomorrow. Scents of the summer coming to a close lingered in the air. Wyler drank it up, glad to be home.

At 2:10AM, the front door of the club opened. A wave of hot, stale air escorted Ellie out. Her head was tilted down, rummaging through her purse.

"Excuse me, Miss," Wyler said. "You wouldn't be able to help a boy and his dog, would you?"

She looked up with a momentary flash of annoyance. When their eyes met, her face softened. Ellie smiled and then laughed lightly, dropping her arms to her side. Blackjack's tail wagged at the sight of her.

"Go ahead," Wyler said to him.

Blackjack leaped at Ellie and rubbed against her legs, not letting her move further without petting him.

"There's my boy," Ellie said, crouching to hug and pet him. "I know it must have been miserable without me."

She stood then and glided to Wyler. His heart missed a beat.

"You're back earlier than I thought," she said. "Is that a good thing or a bad thing?"

Wyler shrugged. "Seeing you feels pretty good to me."

"Oh, what a charmer," she laughed again. "I'm glad to see you didn't run away with a younger, hotter little waitress out in the desert."

"Such a woman doesn't exist."

They hugged, then found each other's lips. When they parted, Ellie whispered. "I missed you."

"Me too," Wyler whispered back.

Ellie pushed away then and playfully punched Wyler in the chest. "And how dare you make me admit that."

Wyler smiled. "How can I make it up to you?"

She grinned. "I've got a few ideas."

Ten hours later, Wyler held Ellie tight in his arms. Sunlight spread through the bedroom windows, cascading them in a warm afternoon glow. He could tell she was awake and was debating saying something. They hadn't talked since he met her outside the Whitmore club. The early morning had been spent reacquainting their bodies, then drifting into a heavy sleep.

"So ...?" she said.

"So."

"What happened out there? Why are you back early?"

"The weather didn't suit me."

"Clearly." She lightly ran her fingers over a patch of healing skin on his forearm. "There's this great invention called suntan lotion, you know?"

"I'll have to look into that."

"So ... out with it. The truth this time."

"Is that what you want?"

"Way to put my mind at ease." Ellie hesitated as she caressed his chest. "Yes, that's what I want."

After talking with Mya and his time spent cooking in the desert, Wyler decided to tell Ellie everything if she asked. Shove all in and let the cards fall where they may. There were no sure things in the world of gambling. Every action was a risk. And the outcomes were simple. You either won or lost. In either case, you could either cheat or play the games straight. To Wyler, keeping secrets was like cheating at cards. You might win, but it's tainted. And the truth would always be there, never letting him forget. Exposing all of himself to her was a risk. But he wanted her in his life and was willing to face that head on. And if he lost, at least he'd have done it straight up.

Wyler inhaled deeply, then exhaled. "Someone tried to kill me. Twice."

She laughed. "Come on."

When he didn't respond, Ellie propped herself on her elbow and stared into his eyes.

"You're serious?"

Wyler nodded.

"Why?"

He took her through everything that happened, leaving little out. When he finished, he studied her face for any tells of what she was thinking.

"That's insane," she finally said. "You know that, right? Like I thought you would tell me you were sleeping around, not stealing dogs from a real estate developer in a battle with someone connected to the mob."

"I know."

"Should I be worried? Will people be looking for you?"

"You're safe ... I'll keep you safe."

"That didn't answer the question."

"I don't know is the short answer. I don't believe so, but I have friends ... helping me to find out for sure."

She shook her head, thinking of what to say next. Ellie bit her lower lip, then whispered, "Did you kill anyone?"

It was the question he dreaded the most. Part of him hoped she wouldn't ask, but there it was. His breathing picked up. He felt like he was inside a vacuum sealer, and the air was just about gone.

Wyler nodded. "In self-defense."

Ellie hesitated. Wyler could tell she was debating the next question. Her gaze never left his face as she said, "And you've done ... *it* ... before? Overseas, in the Marines?" She blinked, looked away, then looked back. "And ... not overseas?"

Wyler swallowed hard, then nodded again.

"And they were people like the ones in Vegas? Bad people?"

"Yes."

Blackjack hopped onto the bed and rolled on his side in front of Ellie, exposing his stomach for her to pet. She scratched Blackjack's chest and stomach. A sad smile eased across her face.

"Was that how he got hurt?" Ellie said, referring to Blackjack.

"Those were bullet wounds, weren't they?"

"Yes," Wyler rubbed Blackjack's head. "That was to help more dogs, too."

"Is this a regular thing for you?"

"I didn't think so, but now ... I don't know."

"Why are you telling me all of this?"

"Because you asked."

She arched an eyebrow and frowned. "No. That's not it."

He sat up, resting his back against the headboard. He stared out the window. "I love you, Ellie Sloan." He looked at her then. "But you have a right to know who I am. What I am. And what I've done. If this is all too much for you and you want to leave ... I understand. Frankly, I wouldn't blame you in the slightest."

"Jesus, do I know how to pick 'em." She wiped a light mist from her eyes. "I thought I had misheard you when you left me that message ..." She continued petting Blackjack. Her silence filled Wyler with dread. He wanted to know what she was thinking but wanted to give her the time she needed to process everything he'd told her.

"My dad used to hit my mom." A far-off look covered her face as she gazed out the window. She stroked Blackjack mindlessly. "We were living in Massachusetts. I was little. Six or seven. He hated himself and took it out on her. This went on for a good two years."

"I'm sorry."

She kept talking as if she hadn't heard him. "Anyway, one day, we're in our shitty little backyard filling up a kiddie pool. He comes home and flips out. Starts screaming about wasting money on water. Goes into a rage and starts in on my mom. Something tripped in me then, some sort of kid defense mechanism or some shit. I grabbed a garden hoe my mom kept out there and swung."

Ellie paused as if the memory were playing against the window only for her. Wyler waited silently for her to continue. The cawing of seagulls ceased as if they had stopped somewhere to listen in to her story.

"It was one of the luckiest swings in the world. I caught him just right in the back of the head. He pitched over and landed right in the pool, face down. Knocked him unconscious. My mom was in a daze from the beating, leaving just me and him. If I left him, he would've drowned, and that would've been that. I wanted to leave him there ... I wanted to so badly ... do nothing ... the easiest thing in the world. But I didn't. I turned off the water and uncorked the pool. While he was still out, Mom and I packed up our few belongings and left. We came here, lived with my uncle, and never looked back."

Ellie pushed some hair behind her ear. "I think everyone is born to carry a certain amount of weight. Do you know what I mean?"

Wyler nodded.

"And if you try to carry more than you're supposed to, it collapses on top of you. I couldn't carry that weight, but someone like you ... were built to handle that type of heaviness. Whether that's good or bad, or right or wrong ... to me ... the world needs people like you."

She looked at Wyler and gave him a sad half-smile. "I guess what I'm trying to say is that I'm glad you were honest with me. It means a lot that you trust me with that information. I get it."

Wyler said nothing, waiting to see if she bolted or stayed.

"So what now?" she asked.

"That's up to you."

Ellie massaged the top of Blackjack's head between his ears. "I think you promised me a vacation."

Wyler allowed himself a slight smile. His heart ached at that moment. Only time would tell if she would truly accept him and what he'd done. For the time being, though, he'd take her response as a sign of sticking around.

"I heard Alaska's nice," he said.

She leaned over and kissed him. When she pulled back, her gaze penetrated deep into Wyler's eyes. He felt like she was staring straight into his soul. When she spoke again, it was soft.

"I love you, too ... just ... don't break my heart, Wyler."

He placed his palm on her cheek and kissed her back, then said, "I won't."

Epilogue

Three weeks later, an ultra-sleek jet touched down on a private runway at LAX. The oval exit hatch opened. Wyler emerged through the small doorway with Blackjack at his side. As Wyler descended the steps, he slipped on a pair of aviators to block the California sun. Twenty feet away were two vehicles. One was a black Range Rover with tinted windows. The other was Wyler's Bronco. Arlo's head of security, Zion James, got out of the Range Rover and walked over. Zion was a compact black guy with forearms as thick as footballs. He was dressed nicely yet efficiently. If a fight broke out, the clothes wouldn't restrict the man from landing a roundhouse kick while being fashionable enough to attend a meeting at a posh restaurant.

"How was the flight?" Zion said, holding out his hand.

"I understand why Arlo enjoys being rich," Wyler said, shaking the brick-sized hand.

"One of the many perks."

"The groveling I had to debase myself with though to get on it ..."

Zion grinned.

"Any issues getting it?" Wyler asked, nodding at the Bronco.

"No." Zion shook his head. "It was right where you said it'd be. My guy said towing it out of there wasn't a problem. It's been charged for you, too."

"I appreciate it." Wyler cleared his throat and looked at Zion. "And Arlo said you had updates for me?"

"That's right." Zion turned when the jet closed the door. He slowly started back to the vehicles. "The remains of a detective—Joel Amos—were found in the bunker at Ortega's. He was linked to multiple corruption charges, and a snitch confirmed he was on Ortegas's payroll. The assault charge was tracked down to some guy named Aaron Gomes. After some pressure, he admitted to being paid to make the phony call. So the BOLO and any charge associated with you is gone."

"Alright." One thing down, Wyler thought.

"In regards to Javier Herrera. The autopsy report contradicted the original suicide narrative, I'm told."

Wyler held his breath and waited. Of what happened in Vegas, he stood to lose the most from what happened to Javier.

"But I'm also told," Zion continued. "The lawyers representing Ortega influenced the report to remain a suicide. Apparently, his team didn't see being attached to a murder, considering the number of other charges he's facing, as beneficial. Your name didn't appear in any reports related to the case."

Wyler exhaled and nodded. He would remain a free man.

"And what about Ortega?" Wyler asked.

"He's been indicted for running an illegal dog fighting ring and building the bunker without proper permits. Some of that will get knocked down, but the other body, your friend Soto, is causing bigger problems. Word is Ortega's second in command, Tenoch Parrada, is getting pinned for the murder. He's facing a life sentence, and we're told, based off of his priors, that it's a pretty open-and-shut case. He's going away for a long time."

Wyler's chest tightened, remembering the pain from the taser. Faint-clicking sounds from the device echoed in his ears. He took some satisfaction in knowing the man with those burning hate-filled eyes would never be roaming free again.

"And there were some lower-level guys found in the rubble of the bunker. Only one of the men survived," Zion said. "The investigators aren't really sure what happened with them. Their wrists were zipped tied together. They think it was a robbery of some kind. The one guy who survived was wanted for past offenses, so he agreed to cooperate with the government against Ortega. Taken together, it's not looking great for him. He is wealthy, though, and has some connections. So he may get out of jail time, but his business will be crippled, and he'll be tied up in litigation for years to come."

"And what about Soto and his family?" Wyler asked, then looked away.

"It's been taken care of per your instructions. The address of where the funeral is taking place is on the dash."

Wyler nodded. "That's everything?"

"That's everything."

"Thanks for the updates. And thanks for the ride."

"Thank Arlo, not me," Zion said, taking his keys out of his pocket. "You good?"

Wyler nodded again and shook Zion's hand. "I'll see you around."

Zion got in the Range Rover and drove off. Wyler opened the door to the Bronco, and Blackjack hopped in. After turning the vehicle on, Wyler rolled down the windows and sat there momentarily, processing everything Zion told him. Relief was there. Wyler was clear from Ortega's entanglements, had saved ten dogs' lives, and doled out justice to evil men. Yet he couldn't entirely remove the pang of guilt lodged behind his heart. Picking up the Bronco was only part of the reason for being in Los Angeles. The other reason was to make good on the promise he made to himself when he was stretched out in the desert facing death. He swallowed the lump in his throat, shifted into drive, and set off for the cemetery.

It was a nice day for a funeral. Big, slow-moving clouds drifted through the saturated blue sky, casually observing the proceedings below. The buzz of insects joined in with the serenading of robins. Wyler sat in the Bronco forty yards away from the burial site. Twelve or thirteen people stood in a loose grouping with somber expressions as the priest read from a Bible. Hospitals and cemeteries were the two places Wyler hated the most. Each place had its own relationship with death. The concepts of cemeteries always baffled Wyler. Burying people beneath your feet left him unsettled. He wasn't religious, but he could never shake the chill that ran through his bones as he stepped on top of people's final resting places. Walking through a cemetery was like walking through a field filled with landmines. When his time came, he wanted to be cremated and scattered to the wind or buried in the soil beneath a tree.

Standing at the front of the mourners were Soto's parents. The resemblance between father and son was uncanny. It was like staring at someone who'd stepped out of a time machine. Grief lined his face. Even from the distance Wyler was at, he could see the puffiness around the man's eyes. The attendance numbers of a funeral were another aspect Wyler found interesting. They showed how many people you had touched meaningfully throughout your lifetime. Where was that threshold of what was considered a good turnout? Zero was the worst-case scenario, obviously, but what about one? Two? Three? If only one person showed, but it was a deep connection filled with years of love and friendship, did that count for more than fifty shallowly connected people? How much was too much? When did it become a gaudy spectacle instead of a somber remembrance?

The priest closed his book, along with Wyler's meandering thoughts. The family stepped forward, touching the American flag draped over the casket. It would be the last time a father and mother would ever be that close to their son again. 'Parents weren't supposed to bury their children' was the common phrase uttered at many a military funeral. Soto's parents had a body to put in the ground, though. It wasn't much consolation, but at least Wyler had given them that. He afforded them the chance at some small degree of closure, which they otherwise wouldn't have gotten had Wyler ended up beside their son in the grave out in the desert.

Two men dressed in formal Marine attire solemnly folded the flag and handed it to Soto's mother. She accepted the triangle of stars and stripes with one hand while the other dabbed a tissue to her eyes. The high polish of the coffin glistened in the afternoon sun. The robins paused their singing, letting the cemetery fall into a respectful moment of silence. Wyler had taken care of the arrangements, paying for everything out of the money Arlo had given him so Soto's parents didn't have to bear the burden. He hoped the gesture meant something to them. And as Wyler slowly eased away, leaving the family to their grief, he knew that part of his heart could harden over now that his debt was paid in full.

END OF BOOK 2

OTHER WORKS BY

MATT DURAND

FOLLOW ME ON:

INSTAGRAM
MATTDURANDUSA

FACEBOOK
MATTDURANDWRITES

FOR MORE VISIT
WWW.MATTDURAND.WORK

LEAVE A REVIEW:

If you enjoyed this book, I humbly ask that you leave a review on Amazon. It goes a long way towards helping the book succeed. My thanks and appreciation in advance.

www.ingramcontent.com/pod-product-compliance
Lightning Source LLC
Chambersburg PA
CBHW020601180626
46810CB00007B/2599